Sembach

SAID SHAFIK

Published by SEMBACH, 2022.

SEMBACH

First edition. September 23, 2022.

Copyright © 2022 SAID SHAFIK.

ISBN: 979-8986992440

Written by SAID SHAFIK.

Disclaimers

The views expressed in this publication are those of the author and do not necessarily reflect the official policy or position of the Department of Defense or the U.S.

Government.

The public release clearance of this publication by the Department of Defense does not imply Department of Defense endorsement or factual accuracy of the

material.

This story is a work of fiction. Names, characters, businesses, events, and incidents are the products of the author's imagination. Any resemblance to actual persons, living or dead, or actual events is purely coincidental.

Prologue:

Scheveningen Prison, The Hague

A particular independent acting unit in Scheveningen prison hosts the United Nations Detention Unit (UNDU), an UN-administered jail, as part of the facility. An elderly inmate stood talking to his legal team in front of the registry office of The International Criminal Court (ICC or ICCt) in The Hague, Netherlands. He looked tired, but his eyes sparkled, and it appeared like a lazy grin played around the corners of his mouth. A court officer walked towards him; age hadn't done too much to reduce his intimidating presence. He met the man's eyes with a calm that unsettled him. With a slightly shaky voice, he called him to come inside the room to hear his indictment:

"Joseph Leonidovich, former president of the Russian Federation, is now ordered to appear before the International Criminal Court."

The older man stared at the officer while walking by him to enter the room. The officer looked like he would bolt, but he didn't. The older man retained the very slight grin just till the moment he turned to face the judge and jury.

The registrar of the Court, Herman von Heber, read to the older man:

"Joseph Leonidovidch, you will appear before the judges of the International Criminal Court, following the actions of the Office of the Prosecutor of the ICC, which conducted independent and impartial preliminary examinations, investigations, and prosecutions of the crime of genocide, crimes against humanity, war crimes, and the crime of aggression. The conclusions found that your case must proceed because it meets the three jurisdictional and admissibility requirements. The three jurisdictional requirements are:

(1) Subject-matter jurisdiction: what acts constitute crimes: You ordered and managed the invasion of a democratic, independent country of Ukraine, committed crimes against its people, and

destroyed its buildings, especially nuclear facilities, that caused severe harm not only to that country's populations but to other countries around it.

(2) Territorial or personal jurisdiction: where the crimes committed or who committed them: While you were president of the Russian Federation, you ordered your army to invade the State of Ukraine. You called your intelligence agency to conduct secret operations against countries sharing the border with the Russian Federation. You ordered the same agency to conduct covert operations to destabilize European societies and cause physical harm to NATO and United States military bases and their civilian and active-duty personnel.

(3) Temporal jurisdiction: Your Russian Army invaded Ukraine on 24 February 2022, in an escalation of the Russo-Ukrainian War that began in 2014. It is Europe's most powerful conventional military attack since World War II."

The registrar turned to the man and said in that still, slightly shaking voice.

"There is a list, the one the Court administrator gave to your legal team, of the crimes you stand accused of Genocide, Crimes against humanity, War crimes, and Crimes of aggression." 's eyes remained still, steady as though they were sown open. Unblinking even in the face of such accusations. He didn't even seem to be in the room, and he stared into space and didn't make eye contact with anyone except when he did.

The old man leaned on his legal team leader and whispered, "I face all that because of a comedian ... and a librarian? To be toppled by those two clowns, I have built the Russian Empire again?" The team leader seemed to smirk. But he didn't give a full smile.

The old man meant the Ukraine president, who was originally a comedian/actor and who resisted the invasion for a long time, supported by the Western allies, until the Russian Generals finally decided to oust the Russian President and agreed to surround him at the International Criminal Court. By saying *a librarian*, the ex-Russian President meant the American systems librarian who discovered the revenge plot to infiltrate and destabilize the European countries and the U.S. military bases in Europe as retaliation for the way they stood by the Ukrainians until the end.

Though the Ukrainian President and the systems librarian never met in person, their brave actions marked the end of the brutal Russian dictator and sealed his fate—to spend the rest of his life in the Hague prison.

The ex-Russian President heard his indictments. Before he was about to walk to his cell, the ICC Prosecutor, Karam Khan, and his two Deputies appeared before him. The Prosecutor asked him: "Do you know where you stand now?" He added: "Let me answer: You are Inside the same building you conspired to destroy by sending your thugs. You failed; thanks to Operation Mitten's heroes who foiled your plot, we will add your attempt to the long list of accusations you face." The Prosecutor then gestured, in disgust, to the guards to take the former president away.

The walk to the cells was short and quiet. The older man walked straight, shoulders squared, and looked like he had no regrets.

An officer was waiting for him by the cell door, holding a book written in Russian.

"Something came for you," the officer said as he handed it over.

"a representative from the capital of the American Embassy in the Netherlands delivered the book, asked to give it to the ex-Russian President himself."

The older man looked at the book with the same blank stare.

"The book is a gift from the United States President; he even wrote a few Russian words on its first page." The ex-Russian dictator took the book from the officer, sat down in a nearby chair, opened it, became very agitated, and gave it to his lawyer. The lawyer opened the book and read loudly:

"I told you many times that you would end up in the dirtiest dumpster of history as the worst dictator of modern times. I told you many times that your end would be in jail, convicted of crimes surpassing what Hitler did during World War II. This book is a Ukraine fairy tale titled The Mitten. Unlike the book you used to include your secret revenge plan codes to your spies in Europe to destroy its societies and the U.S. and NATO military bases, this Ukraine book has no secret codes. Still, I send it to you as a reminder of the many crimes your sick mind and soul committed against the peaceful country of Ukraine and the rest of humanity worldwide."

For the first time that day, the older man looked uncomfortable. He wrung his hands together and bit on the corner of his lips. He would remain there long after his lawyers were gone, just staring into space.

Sembach

In the U.S. military base in Sembach, Germany, the IMCOM (United States Army Installation Management) director, Thomas Meise, walked to the meeting that arranged to congratulate one of its staff, Stacy Wade, for an unusual reason: That staff received from the President of the United States, in the White House, the Distinguished Service Cross (DSC), the second-highest military decoration that awarded only to a member of the United States Army. Meise was a tall, broad-shouldered man with light blue eyes and ginger-colored hair. His brows were thick, and his face had a severe permanent look. He held himself with the rigid and proud stance of a military man, and when he placed his deep blue eyes on people, it felt like he could see into their souls and made them squirm.

In a short introduction of Stacy Wade, a library systems manager in the regional library office in Sembach, Mr. Meise took a long look at the crowd in front of him and then said:

"From the first time I met Stacy Wade, I knew there was something special about him. And I am not surprised that he has always been diligent. But I also noticed that he was attentive and always carried out his duty with great detail. A friend in the FBI once joked with me about recruiting Wade, and with what has happened now, I do not doubt that he will attempt to make do with that playful threat. We all know we won't let Wade wade away from us, though." The crowd laughed as they appreciated the play on words. Most of them had never seen Meise smile, much less make a real joke.

"We gather today to congratulate this man on this honor bestowed by the president. Let all attendees rise and give a standing ovation to the staff."

Every man and woman in the room stood up to honor the man. But, in the far-left corner of the crowd was Andy Walker, green with envy and wishing not too covertly that the honor was his. He worked with Stacy Wade in the same office as a librarian. However, nobody paid much attention to him, as they were too busy showing their love and support for the hero of the hour.

"Wade, I would like to invite you to tell the attendees how your heroic story started and what led you to discover the most dangerous Russian spy operation of the century." The director requested proudly. Wade stood up and walked over to the podium with a slight smile, waiting for the room to become silent before he began talking.

"I want to start by thanking everyone that came out today. It is an absolute honor to be in the same space with all of you" walker rolled his eyes at what he perceived as sugar-coated faux humility.

"I thank my wife, Briza, and amazing boys who have made life a joy for me, and my brother Steven; and his wife Norma—and finally, I'd like to thank the President of the United States for this amazing honor." The room was silent as everyone had settled in to listen to him recount his story. Even though there had been rumors about what Stacy did, they all knew that nothing would substitute for hearing the story from the mouth of the hero.

"I was sitting at my desk one cold February, attending a mandatory online training on anti-terrorism that I had to take every year. My supervisor entered the room and told me to finish the training as soon as possible and prepare for my upcoming TDY (Temporary Duty Orders) to tour the U.S. Department of Defense (DoD) libraries in Europe. I was supposed to create a report on the new unified library system that would integrate all the DoD's libraries under one system. I remember that Lt. Walker asked if he could participate in the tour and questioned why I was the only one selected to go. My supervisor explained that I was a part of the DoD team in charge of unifying the systems of all libraries into one. He added that librarians are not needed at this point..." his voice continued to fill the room with the elaborate tale of how he came to be the most celebrated man in that hour.

The Library Regional Office in Sembach consisted of a director, two technology assistants, two librarians (Andy Walker and Sue Cox), and an acquisitions librarian (Krystyna). The Office functioned as a hub that received all books ordered by European MWR (Morale, Welfare, and Recreation) and NATO libraries from vendors, cataloging them and then shipping them to the proper library. Sue Cox was in charge of training librarians, especially the newcomers, in Europe. She organized online training programs and three in-person sessions every year, bringing all library managers and supervisors to Sembach for four training days. On the opposite side of Andy Walker, Sue was a fan of Stacy Wade. When she learned about Stacy's upcoming recognition and awards ceremony, she invited all European library managers to attend an urgent meeting. One of those managers was Lisa Ortiz, director of Brunssum library, located in the U.S. Army Garrison Benelux. That library provides support to meet the particular international and joint environment demands for military communities in the Netherlands, Belgium, Luxembourg, France, the United Kingdom, and northern Germany. Lisa Ortiz met with Stacy on many occasions when he started his duties, and she also traveled to the area. Lisa was his guide, introducing him to staff and touring the facilities with him. While taking him on tours all over the Netherlands, she fell in love with him. Knowing he was married and single, she kept things to herself.

Days later, the same envious Andy asked Stacy if he could bring his wife, Ann, to visit him in Stacy's apartment to see him off and to ask him to purchase some items from the countries he scheduled to visit. At Stacy's apartment, Ann started working on Briza's ears, telling her to be careful not to lose her husband, who would be alone for a 15-day trip to many European countries and might meet beautiful women. She recommended that they rent the classic movies *The Guide for the Married Man* and *Fatal Attraction* to see what schemes could be cooked up by innocent-looking, happily married men. She added, as instructed by her husband that it might be in the best interest of Briza to convince her husband to take Andy to go with him during the trip.

Ann Walker loved to gossip and always claimed she knew all the latest news. She worked as a daycare teacher in the Kleber Kaserne Child Development Center (CDC). Originally from Alabama, she was known for her recognized southern accent, jokes, and her love for children. Ann was an expert in childrearing, even though she never had any of her own. She had her first encounter with Briza when she met her at the CDC entrance when Briza came to apply for a supervisor position at the Center. Though Briza did not get the job, their relationship continued on and off, especially when they met inside the Exchange Mall in Ramstein Air Base.

Briza was the fertile soil that received the seeds of Ann's lies. If nothing else, this was a good tie for Briza to remember that her husband had been acting the past few days strangely. Stacy always worked on his computer and neglected his favorite and oldest son's requests to go out with him or even to answer some of his questions, which he loved. Could this be the telltale beginning of wilder situations in her marriage? How would she keep tabs on her husband now that he would be away on a trip across Europe for 15 days? Being the rational woman she was, she questioned whether she was unnecessarily riled up and if there was even something that made her worry. What she did not ask was whether or not Ann's intentions were pure and whether Ann's theories applied to her relationship with her husband. She promised to try to convince her husband to take Andy with him on the trip, though she doubted that her husband would even listen to her.

The bond between Stacy and his two sons, Omar and Robert, especially the oldest one, Omar, was strong and got stronger as they grew. Omar's name came up while Briza and Stacy were watching the movie "Dr. Zhivago," starring Omar Sharif, which was about life in Moscow during the Russian Revolution of 1917. They liked the word Omar and decided to make it the name of their first child.

Omar was in his last year in the military high school. He loved sports, played on the high school football team, and traveled with the school to many U.S. military bases in Europe to play against high school teams there. Stacy never missed any of his son's games. His son loved to talk with the father about his passion for becoming a successful businessman and starting his own company. Both used to sit for hours discussing the world of business. Omar was very popular in his school, made lots of friends, and traveled all over Europe with them in his car. Sometimes, the oldest boy brought some of his close friends to the apartment to play on the Xbox. He allowed Robert to share the games. One of those close friends was Konstantin, the son of the Russian housemaster of the building they lived in, Pavel Arseny.

Robert, Briza, and Stacy's younger son rarely left the apartment. He underwent severe spine surgery in the Koln hospital and had to stay home for recovery. Robert's surgery had been a battle Briza had to fight with her husband to spare time to care for his family. Stacy was about to go on a tour of duty to upgrade the library system and train librarians on its new features when Koln hospital sent the date of Robert's surgery.

As Stacy packed his bags that evening, his wife entered the room and leaned against the door.

You can't mean to tell me you intend to go on this trip. Your son needs you!" she said.

"My son needs a loving parent to be with him and another to go out and bring the bread, and he is lucky to have both."

"You are leaving me at a critical time when I need you most!" she wailed. Stacy threw her a glance and shook his head.

"I can't believe you will say something like this to me. You know I feel guilty about this, and it kills me not to be here for Rob," he said.

"No, it doesn't. From what I can see, you are making a choice."

"I am doing my best, Briza... I will sign all the paperwork with the hospital and the insurance company." He said sadly.

"This is not fair. At this time, you should be by your sons' side like a good father. Especially when the hospital would allow more than one parent to accompany Robert and stay with him during the surgery and the recovery after that."

"I have arranged for Islam Ramzan, our Chechen neighbor, to take you and Robert in his van to the hospital on the day of surgery. Then when I came back from my tour, I don't think I'll be back in time to pick you guys up from the hospital either, but I'll be home as soon as possible." She had looked at him as though she was sure he had gone crazy.

"You won't even be here to get us home?" she asked angrily.

"Babe..."

"don't call me baby. You are telling me that you won't be there for your sick child, and now you call me babe?" she was all flushed and seemed ready to burst in his face. But she took a few deep breaths and tried to calm herself.

"Well, at least find someone else to drive us; Islam drives like he has the devil on his shoulders and speaks only Russian."

"Are you being intentionally difficult, Briza? Can't you see that I am literally on my way out now, and there is no time to find someone else?" he asked. She started to say something, but he cut her off as his anger was now palpable.

"I have invited Islam's son, Aslan, to come to the apartment to plan the trip with you and give him the money I agreed to pay his father to drive them to Koln."

"Aslan barely speaks English, Stacy! He only speaks German, Russian, and broken English."

All the better for him to not bother you too much." He said to his wife as he zipped his bag and walked past her at the bedroom door. Just then, Aslan knocked on the door. Briza walked over and let him in. she didn't like him very much. He had pressured Stacy into teaching him how to join the American military; Stacy had given him a link to the U.S. military site designed for local European nationals to apply for jobs within the many different NATO and U.S. bases. Aslan could not apply for any of those available jobs because his family members carried the same travel documents from when they escaped the Chechen war in 2007 and were not able to gain German citizenship since then.

Presently, Aslan and Stacy left the house. He left behind an unhappy Briza, who watched them go from the window. She wasn't sure how she would cope without her husband by her side at a time like this, but Briza knew that when duty called, there was nothing she could do about it. It was love for his country first in her home. It was how it had always been. Aslan sat in the car as they drove towards the airport. Many different things ran through his mind, chief of which was the life he had come from and the life he now had. Ramzan's Chechen family was one of the hundreds of families that arrived in Germany during the 2008 wave of refugees coming from the Chechen-Russian war zone. He remembered clearly that the German government had ordered many schools to empty their guest houses and make them available to host some families. The German local authority gave Ramzan's family the primary school's guest house, located in front of the building where Stacy's home was. Even though he had worked for the military for so long, Stacy had no idea he was dealing with a significant Chechen operator related to the famous, notorious Chechen Ramzan clan that controls the Chechnya Republic of Russia.

2.

Robert was a freshman in the same high school as Omar. The school arranged for him to take all his classes online. As a result, his classmates and friends used to visit him, help him with his homework, and sometimes play Xbox. One of those classmates was a girl his age, Valentina, who constantly flirted with him even though it took him quite a while to recognize or acknowledge it, many of the things high school girls do. She would giggle at his bad jokes, tapping him playfully on his arm. Her parents were a German mother, Daria Kirill, and a

Russian father, Dmitriy Kirill. Valentina spoke German, Russian, and English fluently, so they got along quite well. Because her mother was a German, or "local national," a known expression in the military communities, she got a job at the Army Kaiserslautern Housing Services Office on Kleber Kaserne. That's how Valentina was allowed to attend military high school.

Days before the big day of Stacy's departure and Roberts's surgery, the German-Russian girl Valentina asked her parents to go and visit the ill Robert to show their support. When they arrived, Stacy was not in the apartment; Briza and her sons hosted the girl and her parents.

While Valentina went to Robert's room to chat with him, Omar excused himself to leave for the gym. Briza, Ann, the German mother, and her husband sat around a table on the patio to have tea and refreshments.

Valentina's family had only been there a few minutes when Ann Walker appeared unexpectedly and joined the group. After talking about everything else that came to mind, the conversation inevitably shifted to work. Briza said with a carefree attitude.

"I think being a mother to these two boys is more than enough work. My husband brings home the bacon, and I just make sure it doesn't burn before it gets to our plates."

The group laughed. Feeling encouraged, Briza added.

"I mean. It can be uncomfortable when Stacy reports for duties, but I always remind myself that this is how our family works, and I am comfortable with that."

Valentina Kirill's mother, Daria, nodded and smiled.

"I enjoy working. More than anything and staying home would bore me to distraction." She said. She then talked about her job at Kaiserslautern Housing Services Office on Kleber Kaserne. It all sounded attractive to Briza, but what stood out to her was the fact that she realized that Daria had access to the maintenance arm of her office. Seeing as she needed some work around the house, she seized her opportunity and asked her for a favor to send someone from the maintenance staff from Daria's office to fix her family's dryer.

"Sure. That is no problem at all." Daria said. "I'll have a team replace everything you need to replace." She said. Briza was surprised, and she thanked Daria profusely.

"Wow... that's amazing; thank you so much." She said. At that moment, Ann Walker intercepted the conversation,

"I also have appliances that need replacement, you know; I would appreciate it if you could extend this goodwill to me, too?" she asked.

Dimitri Kirill turned to his wife and nodded to her, non-verbally asking if it was OK for her to help Ann. Daria understood the gesture and nodded in agreement.

"I'm sure there is room to cater to one more person," Dmitriy Kirill told her.

"Just contact my wife Daria in her office tomorrow, and she will take care of you."

Mrs. Kirill then turned to Briza and asked.

"What does Stacy do for a living any way? Why isn't he here today.?"

"To the best of my knowledge, my husband managed the system of libraries of the U.S. Army; in fact, I believe that he will be in charge of managing a unified system for all U.S. Department of Defense libraries." Briza did not see it then, but the German woman and her Russian husband looked at each other and nodded. Ann, who loved to gossip, didn't notice any of these.

She started her news bulletin by talking about

"You know, they are saying that the new wave of troops coming from the U.S. to join the NATO activities is challenging to manage.

"How is it hard for her to deal with the troops?" Dmitriy asked her as he looked at his wife, Daria. "Well, they come with their families, unprepared to be integrated with the military community," Ann said that

"And to make matters worse, their children cannot adapt to their new lives in Germany." "I'll like to step outside to smoke a cigarette," Dmitriy said. The ladies waved him off and continued with their conversation.

Outside, Dimitri found a quiet place and called his field supervisor.

The conversation lasted just a few minutes, but he achieved his goals. Dimitri received explicit instructions: "Continue work on Ann to get more information about the situation in the area." The supervisor added, with a laugh, that they found many people like Ann all over Europe. The latter voluntarily provide information about NATO movements and U.S. military base conditions, while they think it is harmless gossip. He thought of an old-World War II poster he saw on a website. The poster read:

Loose Lips Might Sink Ships

The poster showed a battleship slowly sinking . . . into the sea . . .

He knew that these loose lips were going the sink the ship. And he was prepared for the work up ahead. He knew that he must strengthen his family's relationship with Stacy's family, as she would be an excellent tool to achieve their group's goals. He also knew that Ann Walker could be used as a tool in that matter, considering her "special networking talents." his wife agreed.

Domestic Disturbance

Omar's involvement in one of the world's greatest love stories with Zlata, the third-floor neighbor's daughter, started with a political argument about the war in Ukraine. It developed fast when the two shared the same views regarding Russian aggression. Zlata, who attended a German high school, met Omar one day in the building's garage when he was about to get in his car with his friend Konstantin. She heard them arguing about the war in Ukraine. Once she noticed that Omar was expressing his point of view and taking the Ukrainian side, she approached them and shared Omar's support of the Ukrainian side. Omar was not surprised by her stand because he learned from his father, Stacy, that Zlata's mother was of Ukrainian heritage. Omar knew at that moment that his heart liked her: her long blond hair, blue eyes, and beautiful pert nose. But more importantly, he picked her strength of arguments, her presentation of facts, and her attitude to friendly banter. He knew he wanted to have as much of her company as possible.

Weeks later, Omar and Zlata joined a local warehouse and its attached store, "Hearts for Ukraine," which receives donations to distribute among Ukrainian refugees. Her mother, Roksolana, originally from Ukraine, became a friend of Briza on day one when she came from America. They met during an afternoon walk on the trail near the building. Her husband, Stfan Klaus, worked as a head of the contracting department at Jacobs Engineering in Kaiserslautern and was deeply involved with the center that received and helped Ukrainian refugees to settle in the city. He became Stacy's friend when they met at the Kleber Kaserne in the Kaiserslautern housing office. Stfan was part of the company's team conducting a contract negotiation there. Stacy was applying for his temporary furniture, provided by the Housing Office until he received his furniture shipped from the States. When Stacy told Stfan he had just signed a contract to occupy the first-floor apartment in a building, and, once Stacy mentioned the building address, Stfan said to him that he lived with his Ukrainian wife and daughter in the same building on the third floor. They met on many occasions after that when Stacy or Briza needed advice from the Stfan family.

Stfan, Roksolana, and their daughter Zlata were also involved with the German Society for International Cooperation (Deutsche Gesellschaft für Internationale Zusammenarbeitorganization) which provides internships and aid to Ukrainian citizens, helping Ukrainian refugees settle in Germany.

Zlata often found herself at odds with Robert's girlfriend, Valentina. She always said she considered herself a Russian, taking the Russian party's talking point about the cause of the invasion of Ukraine. One day, they started a never-ending argument, the peak of which had Valentina saying:

"That everyone in America has freedom of speech, and I am just exercising mine" Zlata had looked her squarely in the eyes and said:

"With freedom came responsibility for what you say." At that moment. The two young ladies hated each other almost as much as the presidents of the two warring countries. It didn't improve things; Robert, the youngest son, took his girlfriend's side, as arguments among the four—Omar, Zlata, Valentina, and Robert—Only stopped when Briza intervened.

One day, Valentina brought over some Russian books, translated into English, to share with Robert. One of those books was the Russian fairy tale "Teremok." When Zlata noticed that, she went to her apartment and brought Omar her translated collection of Ukrainian books, including a bunch of fairy tales, one of which was "The Mitten." When Valentina mentioned that her father, Dmitriy, brought with them the original Russian fairy tale collection written in Russian, she had read them many times during her childhood to preserve her Russian heritage. Zlata responded that her mother brought the Ukrainian collection, written in the Ukrainian language, for her to read. She added that her father, Stfan, also got the same collection translated into German.

Days before departing, at the apartment in Kaiserslautern, Germany, Stacy had had to go through rough arguments with Briza and his sons to convince them of the importance of his tour. He promised to go with them on the weekend to visit his brother, Steven, in Belgium, for the boys to see their uncle and for Briza to visit her friend, the brother's wife, Norma. From Belgium, they all would go to Paris for a day trip. Omar said he would arrange with his friend, Konstantin, to drive them for a few hundred Euros during the journey. He added that his Russian friend needed the money because his father, Pavel Arseny, the building housemaster, went back to Russia months ago and has not returned since.

In Steven's apartment in Turnhout, Belgium, they all, including Konstantin, the Russian driver, sat at the dinner table. The talk started with Steven asking how everyone felt and whether the trip was rough. Briza, who was always afraid of speed, said

"My son's friend is good at driving at a reasonable speed."

Steven then asked Konstantin questions about how he got to know Omar and whether driving is his way of living. The Russian explained (feeling insulted)

"I am in the same class in Omar's military high school. Though I am not an American citizen, a completely German citizen, or a local national, my family has the status of temporary citizens with travel documents."

There was a guilty silence in the car for a while, and then he added:

"My three brothers and I attend the military base schools, and we pay a big chunk of our education tuition, and the German government pays a little to support us."

Stacy and his brother were surprised to hear what the Russian driver had just told them, knowing how expensive it was to study in a

U.S. military school for non-Americans. The driver's brothers are also attending military school.

"How are you even able to afford that?" Steven asked.

"All I know is that my father, Pavel Arseny, gets income somehow from Russia, but I don't know where, and we never ask my father those kinds of questions.

"Where is your mom anyway? Why don't you ever talk about her?" Omar asked Konstantin

"I didn't get to know her. Father told my brothers and me that the mother died when we were tiny, and" there was a pause and then he added.

"I don't even remember her face."

"Strange," Omar said.

To change the subject, Steven asked Konstantin.

"Do you know of any relatives or friends in Belgium or France you would like to visit during the trip?"

"I have read much about the "White Russian Émigré" in the history book and wondered if that community still exists."

Steven was surprised to hear such an answer. After 20+ years in Belgium, he had never heard that name. Seeing his shock, Konstantin added:

"The Russians who emigrated from Imperial Russia after the Communist revolution were called by that name." seeing the confusion, he also added;

"There is a new movement among the Russian diaspora in Europe to revive the concept and unite against the current Russian Federation's brutal regime."

Steven agreed with the boy's last statement, noting that unusual activity was underway among the Russian community in the nearby city of Antwerp.

"I participated in a Russian online network called InterNation, where I can communicate with Russians in France and Europe."

Konstantin said, "I would like to visit someone in France; I met her on that platform."

There was silence in the car for the rest of the journey, and everyone was lost in their thought.

In Paris, France, the two families spent the day wandering around, while Konstantin took the car to visit the Russian community in Paris.

On their way back from Belgium, there was still tension between Briza and Stacy. She had spent most of the trip trying to convince him to stay with her and look after their son. Then as a catalyst, he stepped on her toe as he tried to adjust himself in the car.

"Watch it!" she snapped at him.

"Easy there, tiger..." he said as he frowned at her tone of voice.

"Well, at least one of us is being a tiger. I don't know how you are so unprotective of our children." She barked.

"What is that supposed to mean, Briza... I have dedicated the better part of this trip to showing you why I can't give you what you want now. What else do you want from me?"

"I want you to be there for our family... you are never here when we need you." She snarled.

"that's not true." He said with a hurt expression on his face.

"It is too. And you know it," Briza said without looking at him. And before he could counter it at all, she added again.

"I was so ashamed to ask Valentina's mother to send one of her staff at Kaiserslautern Housing Services Office on Kleber Kaserne to fix the dryer. Our family is not taking full advantage of the benefits all civilians who come to work in one of its bases or one of NATO bases in Europe have."

"I have no time to take care of that or anything else until I finish my job tasks."

After thinking a little, he asked Briza

"How did you meet her mother anyway?"

"Valentina brought her parents to see us. Both parents were acting weirdly and asking lots of questions about the nature of your job. They seemed disappointed I did not know much about your career and even said I had a right to know everything. They will be back to visit her and check on Robert.

Stacy thought for a while, noted what happened, and then asked his wife about their names.

"They are a German mother, Daria Kirill, and a Russian father, Dmitriy Kirill," Briza told him.

Stacy told her to invite them on the day he was home. He asked his wife to invite Stfan, Roksolana, and their daughter Zlata, the third-floor friends.

Steven called him the next day when he arrived home, asking about the Russian boy, Konstantin. Stacy was surprised by the line of questioning. When he pressed his brother, Steven said he just wanted that Russian boy's full name, promising he would visit Stacy at home for a talk. He said it was better to meet in person because what he knew could not be discussed over the phone.

"don't come to Kaiserslautern, as the family situation was not good. Let us meet in NATO main library in Brussels during my trip."

"Sure thing," Steven agreed, especially, he said, because he worked as a bus driver for the Brussels Transit Authority, a place that is not that far from where the library is and from where he lived in Turnhout.

Just one day before starting his tour, Valentina and her parents came to the apartment at the invitation of Briza. Stacy ensured to be at home during the visit and warmly welcomed them.

"Would you like coffee in the patio area where we could smoke?" Daria and Dimitri agreed while Valentina went straight to Robert 's room. Minutes later, Stfan and Roksolana and their daughter Zlata arrived. Stacy answered all of Daria and Dmitriy Kirill's questions politely, without showing any suspicion of the queries. From how the woman, Daria, and her husband, Dmitriy Kirill, took turns questioning, Stacy noticed how professional they were in the intelligence business. He memorized all of what they said, their questions, as he intended to write a note about the meeting for his records. After Dmitriy Kirill and his family left, Stfan and his wife, Roksolana, stayed for a while until their daughter Zlata finished visiting Omar's room. Stfan expressed his suspicions about the Kirill family and their behavior, especially that strange line of questions to Stacy. Stfan told Stacy that he would report these people to the authorities if he were him.

MOSCOW

The National Antiterrorism Committee Office

Secret Meetings

Alexandrovich Vasilyevich, Chairman of the National Antiterrorism Committee, presented the situation between the Russian Federation and NATO and the rest of the Western allies after the start of the Russian "special operation" in Ukraine. He suggested retaliating against the actions taken by the West to support Ukraine and its president in resisting the Russian forces.

"Is the plan to include the wake-up of all the Russian sleeping cells all over Europe ready yet?" The Russian President asked. Before anyone could answer, he added matter-of-factly;

"It is time to destabilize those NATO countries, its military bases, U.S. bases, and demoralize Europe's communities, focusing on the 14 countries sharing borders with Russia.

" We can take advantage of the waves of Ukrainian refugees flooding Europe, find ways to use them as a retaliation tool, and make sure to implant Russian agents among them. The latest statistics show that about nine million Russians are in Ukraine, and we have many sleeping cells scattered all over the country, especially in the eastern part of it. We can try to revive some cells in Poland, where there are 13,000 Russians, and in Germany, where there are about two million. The one in Italy is 200,000 Russians strong, and in Turkey, 150,000, in Belgium 20,000, and in the UK 40,000 Russians. Vasilyevich, one of the most potent generals, said to the president.

"don't forget about the Russians in Finland and Sweden." The Russian President reminded Vasilyevich

The room was quiet because the president was not one to be interrupted. They feared him more than they loved him.

At this point, the Russian President asked the chairman

"Do we have enough sleeping cells to do this job?" he asked, suddenly calm from his previous agitation.

"There are enough to do the needed objectives," Vasilyevich responded

"Our Russian sleeping cells are installed everywhere. He added that we have members poised as cooks, grass cutters, soccer officials, contractors, construction builders, bank tellers, military base cleaners, hospital workers, nurses, doctors, airports and railroads workers, and many more places."

"Well... don't forget to include the Chechen group "Kadyrovites" in your plan." The President instructed

The Chairman of the National Antiterrorism Committee was surprised by the President's request. "Mr. President, if I may ask... why do you want to include the "Kadyrovites" in the plan?"

The Russian President smiled and explained

"I worked with the Chechen group since the end of the first Chechen war in 1994, and I know how loyal they are. That paramilitary group name, he explained, was given by Akhmad Kadyrov. When he died, his son Ramzan became its leader and one of the biggest Chechen leaders supporting the Russian Federation."

The President explained why he wanted them to be included in the plan and to play a significant role in executing the operation in Europe: Thousands of Kadyrovites had been dispatched to Ukraine to assist Russian forces alongside the Wagner Group.

"Now," the President said, "I want them to go to Europe and assist in the operation, especially since many of the Kadyrovites were sent to be sleeping cells in Europe long ago." The President added

"There are also about 100,000 Chechen families in Europe, most located in France and Germany, and many are Kadyrovites loyal. Wake up all Kadyrovites and Chechens sleeping cells, and consider giving them major roles in the operation," the President said while standing to leave the meeting. But he was not done talking just yet.

Alexandrovich Vasilyevich, Chairman of the National Antiterrorism Committee, asked the President to issue his order as soon as possible and provide the budget. He added that the security situation at the border countries had been tightened, and it would be harder to include our agents among the Ukrainian escapees.

The Russian President ordered assemble a rapid-action team under the leadership of the head of GRU (Glavnoye Razvedyvatelnoye Upravlenie—the military intelligence service) to start an operation under the codename Teremok, the name of a famous Russian fairy tale. The Russian President's order specifically noted that no activities related to that operation were to take place in any area near and around the harbors and the routes of the NORD Stream 2 project. However, the project stopped after starting the Russian "special operation in Ukraine." "The project can be used as a part of Russia's political game with the Europeans." Then the President turned to Vasilyevich

"Make sure the European Union countries are severely punished for their stand with Ukraine. I originally didn't want to include Finland and Sweden in my list of punishable European countries. Still, since those two countries took the Ukrainian side and applied for NATO membership, they also must be included. As for the situation with Lithuania and this country's block of the Russian exclave of Suwalki Gap and its eponymous capital city of Kaliningrad, you should have that subject in mind when planning the retaliation operation. I'll leave the details up to you, Vasilyevich."

"I use the gas to twist the Europeans' arm and make them change their stand on the conflict in Ukraine." Nobody seemed surprised by this.

"Amongst Europe's major economies, Germany imports around half of its gas from Russia, while France only obtains a quarter of its supply from us. Italy also imports 46 percent of its gas from us; some smaller European countries like North Macedonia, Bosnia and Herzegovina, and Moldova rely exclusively on Russian gas," the President noted angrily.

"Those ungrateful toads think they can spend years leeching off us only to turn their backs on us when we need them the most?" the people in the room shook their heads silently.

"With the dependence of over 90 percent in Finland and Latvia and at 89 percent in Serbia, they think we will sit back and let them enjoy our resources while in the same breath spit on us? They will all feel our wrath." He seemed calmer now, so Vasilyevich took that opportunity to ask.

"Are the economic measure we have taken to enforce the European countries to pay in Ruble enough punishment?" The President smiled and said while he was leaving:

"This is the first step; just keep watching," was when he ultimately walked out of the room.

Vasilyevich summoned the assigned team leader, Valery Gerasimov, the head of GR, for an urgent meeting. He gave him a briefing on the current activities related to the task at hand to establish the retaliation operation and how it was necessary to start communicating with Russian sleeping cells in Europe to prepare them for the process. While talking, he gave a document to Gerasimov, saying it has a detailed report on current and past operations. Valery asked him to provide a brief verbal presentation on previous and everyday activities.

Valery asked more general questions about how Vasilyevich and his team communicated with their agents. Vasilyevich responded that they lately focused on using an old-fashioned way of communication due to the difficulty of running online or phone encrypted messages and considering how active and advanced the counter-intelligence communities in Europe and U.S in tracking and translating Russian communications. He explained that they use special editions of certain books, written in Russian and former USSR states' languages, to communicate with Russian agents worldwide. Valery agreed and said he would build his plan to use the same methods of communication to execute. He suggested adding to it the usage of the digital version of these books to make it easy to access by agents and to be the available backup in case something happens to the printed version. Vasilyevich warned Gerasimov not to make his agents depend on the digital version for fear of exposure.

Vasilyevich said he would first give a presentation on current activities, including the latest preparations for the Teremok operation. He added that an order was placed to one of his agents, a publisher in Latvia, to print and distribute four special editions of a book about Russian fairy tales named *Terermok* (*Теремок* in Russian.) In that edition of the book, an added a chapter with coded details of the operation of demoralizing NATO nations and U.S. bases in Europe. The new editions of the book had been printed and distributed, and he explained that our supreme sleeping agents could include it in the designated libraries in Europe and the DoD military libraries in U.S. bases in Europe. The leading agent who supervised the operation had already picked up the first book. He added that they also coordinated with their agents in publishing houses around Europe to publish three other Russian fairy tale books with new chapters containing the operation's further details. In addition, Vasilyevich explained, one hundred copies of the other three books were printed in Russia and distributed among our agents fleeing Ukraine to Europe as refugees.

Vasilyevich added that the last significant activity was during Locked Shields 2021, a cyber defense exercise organized by the NATO Cooperative Cyber Defense Centre of Excellence. Multiple partners were in cooperation, such as the NATO Communications and Information Agency, the Estonian Defense Ministry, the Estonian Defense Forces, Siemens, Ericsson, Tallinn University of Technology, Cisco, Microsoft, the European Defense Agency, the U.S. Federal Bureau of Investigation, and many others.

Vasilyevich said that some of his agents tried to participate as members of the blue team during the exercises to discover some areas of the NATO system where the Russian cyber-attacking unit might penetrate and cause serious failures, corrupting its data. He added that another team of agents participated in sessions of the "International Conference on Cyber Conflict" (CyCon), organized by NATO. The Conference entered its second decade, focusing on the technical, legal, policy, strategy, and military perspectives of cyber defense and security. He suggested that Valery assemble his agents' team to participate in the upcoming conferences.

"Are the agents able to extract important data from the NATO system?" Valery asked.

"All the information you need is in there," Vasilyevich said as he pointed to the document he handed to him earlier.

"And there is only so much we can do because of the highly sophisticated European security software." Valery understood. He nodded his head in agreement.

Valery Gerasimov assembled a team of nine members for Operation Terermok. In the first meeting, Valery read out the order of the Russian President and gave each member two documents: One had the same goals and details of the plan, and the second had elements of the execution. He distributed four books written in Russian. The members looked at each other, some wondering what they would do with a fairy tale book. Valery explained how the books would be the way of communication between the nine members and all agents and sleeping cells involved in the operation. He then gave the team a week to review the documents and return with their feedback. He emphasized the secrecy of this operation and the documents in their hands.

A week later, the team met in the bunker of the National Antiterrorism Committee. Team leader Valery invited Alexandrovich Vasilyevich, Chairman of the National Antiterrorism Committee, to attend the meeting. Valery wanted to introduce the nine members and hear their feedback after reviewing the documents he gave them.

The team's nine members, Valery told Vasilyevich, are in charge of observing the execution of the plan. Each part of the plan coded is in a specific part of the chapter. Each agent will be assigned a book and will know separately where the chapter is in the book edition. Valery added that each agent would assemble their team and execute their part of the operation. Each agent will not know what the other team members do to guarantee the security of the process. Vasilyevich said he was pleased to meet the team and to understand how prepared they were. He asked that they run a confidentiality test on every one of the sleeping cells before giving any assignments, just in case any of them was discovered, worked as a double-agent, or the sleeping cell changed allegiance to the Russian Federation.

The Operation Terermok headquarters has a sophisticated communication station in a specially designed room. Staff could conduct live communications with agents on the ground, Russian embassies and consulates around Europe, and the Office of the Russian Presidency. They divided themselves into small groups to take shifts, so the particular room could run 24/7 to receive and deliver communications during the execution of the Terermok operation.

DISCOVERY

In preparation for his tour of all DoD and NATO libraries in Europe, Stacy Wade had started visiting libraries in bases near where he lived in Kaiserslautern. He also began running reports of library users, items circulated, and the usage of libraries' electronic resources. Stacy contacted the London office of the company that provided library systems, asking if he could visit and meet with its staff. He had been working with many of those staff on projects related to the Army library systems and on projects related to other libraries he worked for before joining the Army.

Stacy went to Kleber Kaserne to pick up his official passport, issued to those doing business for the government. He then went to the library there to see how things were going. While visiting the base library, Stacy met with the Russian student, his son's friend, and classmate, Konstantin.

He called the lad's attention.

"Hey Konstantin, how are you doing?" he asked with a friendly handshake.

"I'm very well, sir. I'm just visiting my cousin who works at the library, and I need to borrow his Xbox game; my cousin works here."

Stacy frowned at all the unsolicited explanations he was getting; something about the boy was off. Remembering his conversation with Steven and how his brother showed concerns about that student's last name, Stacy decided to ask the student about his last name and the name of his cousin who works in that library. They chatted briefly after that, and Stacy excused himself. He called Steven immediately and gave him the names, confirming they would discuss them when meeting in Brussels. As he left the library, Ann Walker was about to enter.

"Hey, it's nice to see you again, Stacy. You know... the condition of the garrison these days is ..."

"I don't think you should talk so freely about the situation of things on military bases." He spoke.

"It could be dangerous for the officers on base, and you never really know who is listening." He added as a friendly reminder.

"I assume you went through the many securities pieces of training before you were admitted to the base?" he added for full measure.

"Oh, I only ever have such a conversation with known and trusted allies, Stacy. I think you are mistaken in your judgment of me..." she started to say. He didn't budge one bit but just smiled and kept walking.

"Excuse me, I have a meeting now," he said. As he left Ann standing there, he wondered if he should inform the appropriate authorities of her conduct on the base. He sighed. So many dilemmas these days. Ann became very angry and went straight to Briaz'a apartment. Hearing a violent knock on the door, Briza asked Omar to see who was behind that door. Once Omar opened the apartment door, Ann shoved him aside and went straight to Briza with a red-screaming face. She started shouting in her famous Alabama accent, "how dare your husband Stacy tell me to shut up, what he thinks he is?" "He is nothing; my husband is more qualified than him, and you are just a jealous whore who couldn't get the job I have" "I wish you both go to hill" Ann then turned around and burst out of the apartment.

He sat at his computer, frowning slightly at the details in front of him. He had been running the monthly report when Stacy Wade discovered a pattern of checking out or requesting through ILL the specific new edition of a book called *Teremok* (*Теремок* in Russian) written in Russian and published by a firm in Riga, Latvia. He asked his workmate Krystyna, an acquisition librarian in the regional library office, who was in charge of purchasing all items for Army libraries in Europe, how and when she bought that specific edition of the book. Rarely does the Office purchase a new edition of a book of which libraries already have dozens of copies. Krystyna ran a report and told Stacy Wade that the book's latest edition was owned only by a local NATO library. To her surprise, that library held 25 copies of it and made all available for Inter Library Loan (ILL). Stacy and Krystyna were shocked when they examined an ILL report that Krystyna ran on that specific edition. It was heavily circulated among 10 of Europe's NATO and U.S. military libraries. Stacy then ran another report on the people who exchanged that particular edition of the book. To his surprise, all the names sounded Russian to him. An even bigger surprise hit Stacy when he read two names that sounded familiar to him. One of the names was the German woman's husband, the Russian father of Valentina Kirill. The other name was the name of Konstantin's dad, Pavel Arseny.

Stacy searched for the book's specific edition and found results on GoodReads (goodreads.com), a subsidiary of Amazon. He found some comments, in Russian, on that book forum. He then called the local NATO library that purchased the specific edition of the book and learned that the copies were donated by a patron who just dropped them off, asking not to provide his name or any information about him. When he asked the library director about his donation policy, the director responded that there is no specific rule on accepting books or any items donated to the NATO libraries. He referred the system librarian to the NATO libraries policy page, encouraging him to contact the library coordinator at NATO HQ in Brussels, Belgium, for more official assistance. Stacy told the local NATO director that he would be touring all NATO and U.S. military libraries soon and wished to visit his library to meet with him. The discussion, Stacy told the director, would be in person about the matter, asking him to reserve a copy of that edition because he wants to take a look at it.

Stacy asked Krystyna, his acquisition colleague, to contact the book publisher in Latvia and ask to purchase two copies of the new edition of the book. To their surprise, the publisher said that the new edition was out of print, and only 40 copies were made available to the market. He wasn't sure yet how to address the issue on the ground. But he was pretty sure at this point that something was wrong. He didn't want to raise a false alarm, lest he became the boy that cried wolf. But he also knew he had to follow his suspicion and find out what was up with the strange new edition books. So, he slightly altered his trip.

Stacy started his tour in Belgium, continued to the Netherlands, and then to London. He planned to take a copy of the book from the local NATO library director. After visiting the library at the U.S. Lakenheath base in the UK, he would go to London, where he knew a system programmer, Sergey Obolensky, who worked at a company that provides library systems to U.S. Army libraries in Europe. Stacy got to see that person during one of the annual library conferences. Sergey Obolensky was originally from Russia and is now a British citizen. He worked for five years in the presidential palace in Moscow before he immigrated to the UK.

In Brussels, Stacy met with his brother, Steven, and his wife, Norma, in the NATO main library.

"I checked the names you gave me over the phone and found out that some of the people that came on board the public transportation bus he drove daily

"They always act strange and repeat the name of Konstantin's father, moving in groups, speaking Russian, and always carrying bags of the same size and brown color."

Steven added that

"I asked one of my friends who is familiar with the Russian language to sit on the bus with him and listen to them and to try to understand what they were talking about. We found that they were talking in some coded language to such a degree that we did not understand what they were talking about."

Hmmm... how about the names? Did you find anything?

"As far as the names you gave me, I asked Belgium police officers I knew to check on them, we have not come up with any information, and I suspect those are fake names. But I also have a friend who used to work with the Russians and knows his way around their search database, and I'll ask him for help."

Stacy shared his suspicions about the books with his brother, asking him to continue his observations as he might be contacted soon by U.S. intelligence officials.

Stacy complained that scrutiny of the Russian attempts needed to be enhanced, as he met with some people in Europe who were lazy in protecting sensitive information. Stevens' wife, Norma, works at VINCI Energies Belgium, a company that joined other construction companies to build the new NATO headquarters in Brussels. I came over to say hello to Stacy. She participated in the discussion "Despite the continuous emphasis of the company's leaders on the importance of not disclosing any information related to the NATO building, I hear people talking loud while having lunch or just walking on the street about things not should be disclosed." She said. Steven also agreed, saying he heard the same things while driving the bus daily.

In the Netherlands, Lisa Ortiz, director of Brunssum library, was happy to meet again with Stacy. She gave him a tour of the renovated library, showing him the new shelves and the library collection. She gave Stacy a book she thought was unique in her collection, and to his surprise, it was a Russian-language fairy tale. Lisa invited Stacy to her apartment for dinner. They spent the night talking about library issues, had some drinks, and then had coffee. She asked Stacy to stay overnight at her apartment, but he excused himself, claiming he still had a long tour ahead of him, promising to see her again and spend much more time together.

In London, going through the pages of the new edition of the book, the Russian programmer, Sergey Obolonsky, advised Stacy not to try to translate the book but to have an expert in Russian intelligence look at it, as it seemed the book contained encrypted messages on its pages. Stacy showed the Russian programmer the other book he took from Lisa; he was not surprised when the Russian told him it had the same pattern.

Finally, now that Stacy had something to send to the right people, he used his government-secured and encrypted email to send a brief report of his findings to the Chief of staff of Thomas Meise, IMCOM Europe Director. Hours later, Meise himself called Stacy to his office and told him to bring all documents related to his findings. When Stacy entered the Director's room, Meise asked to be left alone with Stacy. After listening carefully to what Stacy had to say and reviewing the documents he brought with him, Weise summoned his chief of staff and ordered him to immediately contact the Office of U.S. Army Counterintelligence in Wiesbaden base, Germany (ACI). That office's primary focus is to identify, counter, neutralize, and exploit hostile Foreign Intelligence Entities (FIE) and International Terrorist Organizations (ITO) targeting U.S. Army personnel and equities and additional joint equities as designated by the DoD. He ordered to save Stacy's documents in a secured government locker; Weise then turned to Stacy and ordered him not to talk to anyone about what happened, not even his direct supervisors and managers, and wait for ACI agents to contact him.

Days later, he was having lunch when his phone rang with an unidentified number calling.

"Hello?" he said into his phone with a frown.

"Is this Stacy wade?" the voice on the other end was stern and authoritative.

"Who is asking?" Stacy asked.

"Keep the file of your findings in a safe place, and a DoD representative will be in contact soon."

Stacy was about to say that IMCOM Director had saved his documents, but the line was already dead. A week later, a Defense Intelligence Agency (DIA) general arrived from Washington, DC, to Sembach. A special agent from the Director of National Intelligence Office (DNI) came along with the general to interview Stacy. They asked the IMCOM Director to take Stacy to a secured place for an interview.

As soon as the door was closed behind them, the general who came with the special agents asked him.

"Wade, why didn't you just report these findings through your chain of command?" he asked.

"I wasn't quite sure how serious my findings were, and I didn't want to spread panic. Also, I didn't want to risk a leak down the chain, so I figured I would get the information as far up as possible without tipping the spies off." He added, "I thought the best way was to go directly to the IMCOM director, knowing that Mr. Weise reads all his emails personally and right away" The general nodded. He seemed impress d by Stacy's foresight.

"well, Stacy, what you found is a serious matter, and for that, all the17 members of the Intelligence Community, led by the Director of National Intelligence Office, will be involved in the investigation of your findings: CIA, DIA, FBI, Marine Corps Intelligence, National Geospatial-Intelligence Agency, National Reconnaissance Office, National Security Agency, Office of Naval Intelligence, Drug Enforcement Administration's Office of National Security Intelligence, U.S. Air Force Intelligence, Surveillance and Reconnaissance, U.S. Army Intelligence and Security Command, U.S. Coast Guard, U.S. Department of Energy, U.S. Department of Homeland Security, U.S. Department of State, U.S. Treasury Department, U.S. Space Force Intelligence. Every single one will require a regular brief and update on the investigation. You'll be required to participate in the full extent of the investigation." Stacy stood there as the man talked on and on.

The interview took more than 11 hours, with short breaks. Stacy gave a presentation, in detail, of his findings. He explained how he started to trace the pattern of behavior related to the circulation of a Russian book, in print and digital formats, among DoD libraries in Europe. Stacy noticed other suspicious activities by some of the NATO countries' local nationals and some Russian-origin European citizens in those countries. He told them he thought the behavior was a part of a worldwide operation run by Russian intelligence. He presented documents to support his findings. Stacy mentioned what his brother Steven told him about Russian groups in Belgium. The DNI agent took Stacy's brother's contact and address information, telling him to inform his brother that an agent would be visiting him soon.

As soon as Steven's name was mentioned, DIA sent a small force to bring him because they needed to hear from him directly, but more importantly, they knew that he might be in danger if anyone knew about the conspiracy.

The general from the DIA arrived in Belgium. A special agent from the DNI came along with the general to interview Steven at the America Embassy in Brussels. Steven repeated to them what he told his brother about the Russian-speaking people that rode with him on the bus and how they used aliases, unusual types of languages, and how strangely they acted. The agent told him they would send a particular CIA operator to ride with him on the bus. Other operators, the agent said, would scan the areas where these people gather and move.

The DIA general, the DNI special agent, and the head of the U.S. Army Installation Management Command (IMCOM) in Europe decided to relieve Stacy from his assigned TDY. He was taken to a secure place until they received instruction from Washington, DC. He was allowed to call his family but only to inform them that he would be away for longer than he initially expected.

That call was short but emotional, and it ended with Briza screaming "I hate you, Stacy" into the phone. For minutes after that call, Stacy sat on a corner bench. Thinking about all the ways he wished he had not discovered what he had.

Days later, the general was instructed to fly back to the capital and bring with him Stacy Wade. In Washington DC, the Director of the National Intelligence Office (DNI) arranged for an urgent meeting, calling all directors of the 17 members of the intelligence community to attend. He invited the U.S. Secretary of Defense, NATO's Supreme Allied Commander Europe, and the head of United States European Command (EUCOM) to discuss the findings of the systems librarian and how to put together a plan to face the Russian threats.

After consulting with his National Security Council members, the Director told the attendees that the President of the United States ordered this meeting. He added that the objective of today's meeting, as the President directed, is to confirm if there are Russian activities to demoralize and destabilize the European and NATO countries and societies and if these Russian activities are aimed at the U.S. military bases in Europe as well.

"The second directive by the President," the Director said

"Is to come up with a plan to counter Russian activities. from now on, and until the President disbands them, we will meet daily to prepare a final report on the findings."

He then asked everyone around the table to assess the situation as each member saw it and how each division planned to participate in a significant operation to counter Russian threats.

The head of the EUCOM showed his concerns about the accuracy of the systems librarian findings, calling for the need to verify each of those findings to the extent that leaves no doubts about them. The Director of the National Intelligence Office (DNI) asked the Secretary of Defense to order a quick review of all that had happened, from the very beginning until the current point, including interviewing all the people involved: Krystyna, the acquisition librarian; Lisa Ortiz, the London programmer; Stacy's brother; and even re-interview Stacy himself. The DNI Director distributed documents to the attendees regarding some ideas about how to counter Russian penetration into European societies.

The documents noted that scattered communities in European cities of Russian descendants oppose the current Russian regime. There are also documents showing the starting appearance of a new wave of social media channels aimed to wake up and support the Russians who live inside Russia and in the eastern region of Ukraine to resist the Russian President's invasion of Ukraine. An example of that is the document mentioned by Ekaterina Kotrikadze. She was the Deputy Editor-in-Chief of RTVI, the independent broadcasting network shut down days after the Russian invasion of Ukraine. Now, from Tbilisi, Georgia, she leads a movement to mobilize the descendants through the YouTube channel where she is the author and Tikhon Dzyadko, with more than 500 thousand of audience.

The DNI director said that the US and allies' intelligence communities ought to contact and support those organizations and websites run by opponents of the Russian dictatorship. He emphasized the need to support sites such as the Forum of Russian-speaking Europeans.

"The aim of the Forum," he said,

"Was to unite native speakers of the Russian language and supporters of the culture living in Germany and other European countries, who were proponents of European liberal democratic values and opponents of the Russian-aggression regime."

"February Morning," he added, "Is a new international Russian-language platform for

Conversations with experts, analysts, and intellectuals, founded by politician and entrepreneur Ilya Ponomarev that we must support, as it aims to educate the Russian public inside Russia, and to encourage resistance movements inside Russia against the war in Ukraine."

The head of the EUCOM commented: "I have a suggestion, but I don't know if it is possible to be implemented." "Let's hear it," Said the DNI director. "Since you mentioned, sir, the word organizations, and I got to know a Ukrainian one that is very active globally, named European

Congress of Ukrainians, my idea is to establish a new global NGO group to unite all these organizations under one umbrella and make its activities a part of the counter operation?"

The meeting was adjourned until the verification was done.

The U.S. Secretary of Defense took the Director of the National Intelligence Office aside and asked him if he could meet privately with Stacy Wade, who started the investigation. The director pointed to the CIA head, saying he was the only one to ask, as the CIA hosted Stacy in an undisclosed location. In the meeting with the Secretary of Defense, Stacy saw his opportunity and asked.

"Sir, if it is not too much trouble, I'd like to meet with my wife and two young boys. My younger son is sick and in need of a review of the surgery he had by his doctor; my wife already hates me for leaving, and I just want her to know that my heart is with them." He explained.

The man didn't seem particularly inclined to grant Stacy's request. So, he went on to tell him the thing that had been weighing on his mind since he last called his family.

"Look, sir, my wife already thinks I abandoned her. She asked for a divorce the last time we talked. And I know the love of country comes first, but my family is all I have. Only a happy and healthy office can serve the country well. I can't lose her." He said desperately.

"This wife of yours must be pretty special," the general said.

"She is," Stacy responded.

"Well, thank you for your heroic work; I assure you that your office (IMCOM HQ Europe) will take care of your family. You have my word."

"Thank you, sir," Stacy said.

"Two important facts, though," The Secretary of Defense explained

"One, you must be kept in a safe place. Second, your wife and boys must conduct their lives as usual and not show any signs that they can be picked up by Russian agents that might be active in the area where they live. As for how long this captivity would last, the Secretary of Defense told Stacy it must continue until the preparation of the counter-operation is over."

"I understand, sir," Stacy said. The Secretary of Defense turned to his aide and asked if the director of the CIA could join the meeting with the systems librarian.

When the CIA director arrived, he told Stacy and the Secretary of Defense that after verifying what Stacy had presented, he wanted him to join a team of his cyber-intelligence experts to run reports. They have to see if there are other fairy tale books with new editions written in Russian and other former USSR states' languages to see if there are different patterns.

Briza was not in a good mood. She had not been since that fateful phone call with a tract in which he told her that he would not be coming home right away. She was angry at how her husband had behaved. She understood that his work might be highly demanding, but she also knew that he had not done enough to communicate with her properly. Just as she was missing over the situation, she heard a knock on the door and went there to check it out.

A young man from IMCOM EU. in plain clothes stood at her door.

"Mrs. Wade?" he asked

"Yes?" she answered.

"I am the chief of staff of Mr. Thomas Weise, the IMCOM EU director. Can we talk?" he asked.

Her eyes lighted up in confusion.

"Please tell me he is not dead," she said with tears.

"No. Not at all. I apologize if I gave you that impression." The staff said.

"I need to see you and your boys in a private space where we can talk quietly." He said.

"Sure... come right in." She said as she led him into the house. She led him to Roberts's room, where she knew they could talk privately without bringing the boy downstairs.

"I am Chief of Staff James Paulson; I have been sent by the Director of IMCOM EU, Mr. Weise, to let you know of a situation with your husband." Briza sat down and braced herself for the worst. Paulson told Briza and the boys that Stacy's mission had been extended and might last longer than expected. Briza became agitated and asked why they were kept in the dark, telling the Chief of Staff she wanted to divorce her husband and take the boys back to America. Paulson tried to be as calm as he could. He explained to the wife and the boys the firm instructions by the authorities to stay in the apartment and act as usual, or they would risk a national security operation. Staff said he wished to give more details but was not authorized to do so. He assured them that Stacy was a national hero and loved them all. He asked Briza to be patient; once she knew all the facts, she would forgive him and admire his sacrifices for his country. As usual, the officer told them that the salary would be deposited, giving his contact information to call him anytime if needed.

Briza was relieved and proud. She sighed a deep sigh of relief for the first time in a while.

"Thank you, sir." She spoke.

"Tell him I love him," she said.

Paulson then contacted Stacy, told him about his visit to his family, updated Stacy on family matters, and assured him they were all in good health, especially the younger boy. He also told Stacy that his oldest boy, Omar, started dating a young girl named Zlata. Stacy was happy since Zlata was his friend Stfan's daughter. He said to himself; *finally, Omar has come to live his age!*

The final verification report arrived at the DNI Director's Office in the middle of March. He then called for an urgent meeting with all directors of the 17 members of the intelligence community to attend.

He invited the U.S. Secretary of Defense, NATO's Supreme Allied Commander in Europe, and the head of United States European Command (EUCOM) to discuss the verification report. The report confirmed all the findings by Stacy, his brother, Krystyna, and Lisa. The report confirmed alarming activities by the Russian National Antiterrorism Committee and its preparation for a full-scale operation to penetrate Europe, NATO, and US military bases and communities. The report added at its end that the Russian operation is called Terermok, after a famous Russian fairy tale.

He then suggested establishing a counter-intelligent operation to foil the Russian attempts and calling the operation: "Mitten," a well-known Ukrainian fairy tale, asking the CIA director and the others. They were involved in starting the preparations for the operation immediately without wasting any time.

Inside the CIA building in the Cyber room, Stacy sat with a team of programmers to discuss how to run reports for all new book editions in all European libraries. "It must be done by the vendors who own the library's systems," Stacy said. The CIA and FBI directors attended the meeting. The FBI director said it must be done with a court order and added that he would take care of it. Still, he suggested that if they needed the library systems vendors' programmers to find the books and who borrowed them, they would need a librarian to assist in finding them in all formats. Stacy, remembering their good times together, suggested bringing Lisa Ortiz, director of Brunssum library, to join them. She was ordered to prepare to fly to Washington, DC, on a special TDY mission without knowing anything about it. When she arrived at the CIA Cyber room, she was surprised and happy to see Stacy. Stacy took her aside and explained to her, in brief, the task at hand and why they needed her participation in that part of the operation.

Each CEO of the 16 library system firms that own and contract their systems to be used in Europe, some of them European-based, received a phone call from the FBI director, notified of the task in hand, and ordered to send one or two of the company's top programmers. Stacy led programmers to run reports of newly published books in Russian, especially those that had new editions and distributed among NATO and U.S. military libraries in Europe. When the CEOs mentioned a possible privacy issue violation, the FBI director assured them that there was already a court order to cover that part.

The needed reports on the books were compiled, ran through special analytic software, and came up with the final result. Stacy and Lisa analyzed the results and narrowed it to specific sets of four books, all written in Russian and circulated in European libraries, the same way Stacy found the book in the local NATO library. Lisa Ortiz told them she remembered noticing some books written in Russian were added to the collection in her library. However, her library never had such books, and she added that her collection consisted only of Dutch, French, German, and English items. Lisa reminded Stacy that she had given him a copy of one of those Russian books when he visited her library during his tour. Lisa added that she also noticed the book record in her collection had e-book and audiobook versions attached to that record. Stacy told her he gave that book and another one he got from the main library of NATO in Brussels, along with its digital editions' information, to the CIA team.

Because of the success of their mission, Stacy decided to go out for dinner in a restaurant on the Potomac River. After dinner, they went for a walk alongside the river before going back to their hotel. Lisa insisted on inviting Stacy to have coffee with her in her room. They ended up spending the rest of the night in bed.

Stacy woke up the following day and found himself in Lisa's bed. He felt guilty. It was his first time sleeping with a woman other than his wife of 20 years. He left the room angry, promising himself it would never happen again, and wondered,

"How will I be able to look Briza in the eyes?

Later that week, the team found an interesting pattern in the narrowed report: Those books with new editions each were published by a different publishing house, and each was located in one of the former USSR republics. The books were written in Russian, all about Russian fairy tales. The FBI director said the urgent task was finding at least a copy of each book. He sent to field operators in Europe and elsewhere instructions to find those copies as soon as possible and to send them through diplomatic channels without bringing any attention.

CIA and FBI directors agreed on the urgency to break the codes in those books and translate the encrypted messages as soon as possible. That's why they sent special agents to the ex-Russian spies jailed in Virginia prison. The CIA director advised them not to give the four books to only one spy to break the codes. Instead, he told the FBI it was better to collect a group of those ex-spies and have an FBI negotiation team deal with them. Translating the codes in all four books must be done as soon as possible, the CIA director said, emphasizing that they do not know when the Russian operation would start and which places it would hit first in Europe.

CIA and FBI directors presented their report on the findings to the National Intelligence Director's Committee meeting. They said they at least have a list of people that exchanged the books between themselves, all located in Europe, in, or near NATO and U.S. military bases. Regarding resolving the codes in the books, the FBI was finding a way to get it done.

The committee's chairman suggested that people on the list should be rounded up and quietly arrested without raising any suspicion that might alert the Russians. This process would speed up the attempt to resolve the book's codes. The CIA director disagreed. He said arresting people would cause the operation to fail. Family members and community activists could go online and post the news of their arrest.

He suggested that everything must go simultaneously, especially after the new information his office received lately about dozens of Russian agents planted among the Ukrainian refugees fleeing to Europe, and some CIA operators reported seeing some of those agents' carrying copies of the same fairy tale book. The CIA director added that there were reports from the European fields of Chechen paramilitary groups infiltrating Ukraine from European countries bordering Russia and Ukraine.

At the end of the meeting, the CIA director asked if there was still a need for Stacy and his colleague Lisa. The chairman told them to check with the Secretary of Defense and let him decide what to do with them. Until the Secretary of Defense made up his mind, the chairman said, just host them in one of your guest houses in DC. Stacy requested to stay in a guest house far from where Lisa stayed.

Operation Mitten

After the President of the United States reviewed the report, he called an urgent meeting of his National Security Council and asked the Secretary of Defense to participate. He ordered an urgent review of security measures of all U.S. military bases in Europe to find any traces of Russian penetration. He added that the U.S. must join with the intelligence community of the European countries to scan for traces of any Russian operators in those countries. The President emphasized that all measures taken should be done quietly, asking the Secretary of Defense for a report on the current Force Protection Conditions. The Secretary of Defense said that out of the five conditions, named Normal, Alpha, Bravo, Charlie, and Delta, the current condition in U.S. military bases in Europe was Normal, adding that he thought it was the same level in NATO bases. The President then ordered not to raise it any higher, not to alert the Russians of the discovery. The President issued an executive order to immediately start the secret Operation Mitten to be led by a special presidential counselor with the code name "Big Bear," a main character in the Ukrainian fairy tale. The President emphasized the importance of assembling the best team to run the operation, instructing to make use of former Russian spies who defected to the U.S. and European countries.

Operation Mitten succeeded before the Russian operation was even scheduled to start.

A team of FBI agents went to the prison in Virginia and asked the director to meet, in private, with a group of Russian inmates. Those Russians were spies caught months back during a U.S. sting operation in Latvia and some other Eastern Europe countries. The spies spoke Russian and other Eastern Europe languages, such as Lettish, Latvia's primary language. The agents asked the spies if they were ready to cooperate with U.S. authorities to resolve an issue involving a Russian book with encrypted messages on some of its pages. Many spies agreed to cooperate when they heard they would get something in return;

others asked to think about it for some time, and the rest refused to cooperate.

The eight Russian spies who agreed to cooperate to solve the book's codes were transported under heavy security to the Cyber Room in the CIA building. Each was given one book out of the four to study and resolve its code. The most experienced of them, Sergei Kouzminov, told the Operation Mitten team that, from his working experience with Russian intelligence, one of these four books must be the one that has the general instructions; the other three books would have details of specific operations. After consultation between the Director of the National Intelligence Office and the CIA and FBI directors, it was decided to take the most experienced Russian spy to a room equipped with unique cameras and voice recognition software and give him all four books to examine. After a few hours later, he asked to meet with the directors. When the three directors entered the room, he presented one of the books, saying he thought this book had the general instructions. He added that he was sure that only one person in the sleeping cells would be able to know what those instructions were after reading the book. When asked if he could resolve that book's code and instructions, the spy told the directors that the task was difficult unless they brought one of the Russian spies, Vasili Butina, from the prison, who told the agents he needed time to consider their offer.

A special agent from the FBI negotiation team went back to the prison in Virginia to talk to the captured spy. The negotiation did not go well, as the Russian spy gave the agent his demands, saying he would not assist in any way until they were all met. He wanted his Russian-Turkish wife; also a spy, captured two years back in Ankara by Turkish Intelligence (İstihbarat Teşkilatı) with their three children, to be released and sent to Israel. Also, he requested that his parents, brothers, and sisters be allowed to emigrate from Russia to Israel to be united with his wife and kids.

The FBI and CIA directors returned to the experienced ex-Russian spy, Sergei Kouzminov, asking him to name someone else, telling him that the spy he named had impossible demands. The experienced Russian spy told them that the guy was the only one they had who was capable of resolving the codes because his job at the Russian intelligence agency was to code similar messages.

The Director of the National Intelligence Office called the President of the United States and explained to him the situation, emphasizing the short time they had to resolve the codes to start the operation.

The U.S. President called the Turkish President to ask him for the favor of releasing the Russian spy and her children. The Turkish President wasted no time in asking for the capture of the Turkish opposition leader residing in the U.S. and sending him back to Ankara to face trial for treason. The U.S. President explained to his Turkish counterpart how hard it was for him to take such an action. The phone call went nowhere. The President then called the Director of National Intelligence, asking him to choose another ex-Russian spy to do the task. The Director explained to the President why they needed that specific ex-spy to resolve the codes, as he used to code messages while working for Russian intelligence. The President then asked the Director to go himself and renegotiate with the ex-spy and explain to him that the Turkish part of his demand was impossible. The ex-spy insisted so the President called the leaders of Congress to the White House to meet him and his National Security team. After a lengthy discussion, a National Security staff suggested a compromised solution: Put the Turkish leader under house arrest, round up his top followers, and make sure to put a cap on the opposition activities against the Turkish leader but not send anyone back to Ankara.

The Turkish President finally agreed after the U.S. president promised to send some military equipment the Turkish continuously asked to receive, but Congress blocked the shipments many times before. The Turkish-Russian spy was then allowed to travel to Israel with her children. When the U.S. President hung up the phone with the Turkish President, he told people around him that the Turkish President was just a pain in the butt.

Regarding the Russian part of the ex-spy demand, things were more complicated than the Turkish demands. The U.S. President had to ask the Israeli Prime minister, who had a good relationship with the Russian President, to travel to Moscow and talk to the Russians because the relationship between the two countries was at its low point after the invasion. The American President had to agree to release three ex-Russian spies in American prisons to have the Russian President agree to allow the ex-Russian spy's family to immigrate to Israel. The U.S. President told people who attended the call that the Russian President would regret his decision when he knew why he freed the ex-Russian spy's family after the spy decoded the messages. Operation Mitten succeeded in stopping the Russian operation before it started.

Once all demands were met, and the ex-Russian spy could call his family in Israel, agents moved him to the Cyber Room to start working with his colleague, the ex-Russian experienced spy, and the rest of the ex-Russian spies on solving the codes.

A week later, the Operation Mitten leader, the Big Bear, invited the Director of the National Intelligence Office to a special meeting to give him a briefing on his team's discovery.

The leader introduced his assistants, the rest of his team members, and a group of ex-Russian spies. He said he would give the first presentation for its importance, and then each one of them will give a presentation on their findings after resolving the book's codes.

First Book: General Instruction – Time

The team leader started his presentation by telling the attendees that the first book was the most important because it was addressed to the supreme Russian operator in Europe and revealed the operation's goal, its name, time, and maps of execution places. The book also revealed, the leader added, the places where weapons, money, and equipment will be used to execute all operations.

The team leader said he would like to mention the reasonable efforts of the ex-Russian spy, who demanded his family to be sent to Israel, for his fast resolve of the book codes, and his efforts to help other ex-Russian spies resolve encrypted chapters in the books they handled.

The leader then started his presentation by reading a translated version of the resolved encrypted chapter in the first book:

In preparation for the possibility of our invasion of a country sharing the border with us, and from our experience with the reaction of Western European countries and the U.S. after the Crimean Peninsula came back to join us, we must execute a plan ordered by the President of the Russian Federation, to destabilize and demoralize European societies and the U.S. military communities in Europe.

How: Four significant operations would be executed all over western Europe simultaneously. Yours is the most important one. This book chapter addressed you, our supreme agent in Europe. No one else will be able to read it or decode it; only you can unencrypt its words. Another 13 agents are reading three specific books at the same time. As a supreme agent, your duties are to observe the execution of the other 13 operations, record the results and feedback of the Europeans and the Americans in Europe, and send reports back to our office in Moscow.

Time: The original timeframe for executing the operations decided by the team leader in Moscow was the first of October to the end of the month, but because of the situation in Ukraine, operations must start immediately. Each agent will report separately to our office in Moscow with secured encrypted messages, and no agent would know what the other agents do. In each book are details of the operation, instructions to the agent on assembling their local team from the sleeping cells, and where to find the equipment, cash, and weapons needed to execute their operation. You will be contacted and ordered to execute one part or more of the operation using your team if needed. That's why we provided you, in Appendix A, with coded maps of the other operations.

As a supreme agent, you must spend the time of the operation traveling, alone, all over Europe, using a different identity when entering each country. Daily reports must be sent to our office no later than 22:00 hours GMT. Do not contact any of our local offices in Europe. If you feel one of the operations of any of our agents is exposed, report immediately, in person, to one of our embassies near where you are. People there know what to do in that situation. As a supreme agent, you know what to do next, as instructed before.

After finishing his presentation, the Operation Mitten leader was about to ask the first ex-Russian spy, the most experienced of them, to present the book he worked was decoding. Still, the National Intelligence Office Director stopped him and asked to meet privately in his office.

When the Mitten operation team leader closed his office door, the National Intelligence Office Director asked him to call the CIA and FBI directors to come in for an urgent meeting. When they arrived, the Director of the National Intelligence Office told them that if the information in the leading Russian book proved correct, he must inform the President of the United States immediately. The Operation Mitten counselor, Big Bear, handed out a copy of the decoded chapter of the book to CIA and FBI directors. After reading the chapter carefully, both directors asked for a few days to verify the information with their local and international stations. The Director of the National Intelligence Office told the directors that he thought the other three chapters would have even more damaging information, so they must act fast.

The Operation Mitten leader then asked the Director of the National Intelligence Office: Should the team of ex-Russian spies resume their presentation, or should they wait for his instructions?

All agreed on the resumption of the presentations, and CIA and FBI directors said they would join after making some phone calls.

Sergei Kouzminov, the most experienced Russian spy, started his presentation by suggesting analyzing the map he found at the end of the chapter because this map has all of what the Russian operators will do and when. On the map, he pointed out ports, rails, highways, EU Headquarters, Rail Baltica administrative buildings, its project locations in five European states, and the storehouses where the sleeping cells would find weapons, money, explosives, and detonators. He then read the decoded chapter.

Second Book: TEN-T

The leader continued his presentation.

Goal: Disrupt U.S. and NATO military mobility

Moving military troops and equipment from point A to point B in a timely fashion can mean the difference between a crisis averted and a war lost. That was the lesson we learned during the Crimean Peninsula crisis of 2014 and the special military operation of 2022 in Ukraine. In Europe, military mobility is incredibly complex since it requires seamless movement of people and equipment across the Atlantic and multiple allied borders. We want to keep it this way and even make it more complex.

How: Your team's role is to disrupt projects, make sure European ports cannot support military mobility, and infiltrate U.S. bases to demoralize its troops. Be flexible when choosing how to achieve your goals in this area, but you must be fast and select special sleeping cells noted at the end of this chapter. At the end of this chapter, you will find the names of the Chechen team we sent to support you and information about its local contact in Europe, Islam Ramzan.

We coordinated with the agents we planted in the new European Climate, Environment, and Infrastructure Executive Agency (CINEA) which is in charge of all open TEN-T projects. The projects represent all transport modes – air, rail, road, and maritime/sea – plus logistics and intelligent transport systems and involve all EU Member States. Disrupt all these projects.

Also, focus on disrupting Rail Baltica, a greenfield rail transport infrastructure project to integrate the Baltic States into the European rail network. The project includes five European Union countries – Poland, Lithuania, Latvia, Estonia, and, indirectly, Finland. It will connect Helsinki, Tallinn, Pärnu, Riga, Panevežys, Kaunas, Vilnius, and Warsaw. The Baltic part of the Rail Baltica project is referred to as the Rail Baltica Global Project. Equipment, money, communication tools, and weapons are stored where you had been told before. Use the Chechen special force "Kadyrovites" to attack U.S. military bases in the U.K., especially the Lakenheath base, which has contributed to eliminating drone strikes, the transportation of weapons for military operations, mass surveillance, and destabilizing the Russian missile defense system during the special military operation in Ukraine.

While this task is being executed, focus on disrupting European nations' cyber resilience in telecommunications, electric grids, and transshipment facilities critical to warfighting, including private assets and civilian transport, which are more vulnerable and difficult to reconstitute in the event of a compromise.

The ex-Russian spy said he could resolve these sleeping cells' encrypted names, contacts, and locations. Most importantly, the attached maps with the exact places to be destroyed and the routes the sleeping cells would follow during their operation.

After the lunch break, the Operation Mitten leader introduced the second ex-Russian spy, Sergei Kouzminov, who said he asked Big Bear to work on this specific book to solve its encrypted chapter because he was familiar with the U.S. military community in Germany. He added he was stationed in that area before being exposed, arrested, and transported to the U.S. to face trial and serve prison time. He added he would provide information about his old Russian spy ring, the locations, members, bank accounts, and other information he might remember. He then started his presentation:

Third Book – From Rhineland-Pfalz to Wiesbaden to Rammstein

Goals: Disrupt administrative actions and construction project operations in Germany's U.S. military community. Time: Month of October.

United States Army Garrison (USAG) Rhineland-Pfalz includes 31 sites across Germany's Rhineland-Pfalz region, which includes Baumholder Military Community, Miesau Army Depot, Wilson Barracks (Landstuhl), Germersheim Army Depot, Grünstadt Depot, Rhine Ordnance Barracks (ROB), Pulaski Barracks, Kaiserslautern Army Depot, Sembach Kaserne, Panzer Kaserne, Daenner Kaserne, Kleber Kaserne and Coleman Work Site. The garrison headquarters is located on Rhine Ordnance Barracks in Kaiserslautern. Goals: Operators must interrupt communications between those barracks by destroying their signal units.

U.S. Army Garrison Wiesbaden The home of U.S. Army Europe and Africa Headquarters, servicing 15 installations and housing areas in and around Wiesbaden, including the Clay Kaserne, Dagger Complex in Darmstadt, a housing area, and training site in Mainz and McCully Support Center in Wackernheim. Goals are to interrupt all services, focusing on its intelligence offices.

NAU - U.S. Army Corps of Engineers, European District: Goals are to interrupt and destroy its current projects, including the design and construction of family housing communities at Wiesbaden, Vilseck, and Baumholder and Ansbach, Germany; and Incirlik Air Base, Turkey. Maps are included at the end of the book chapter.

Military Hospitals: There is a major large medical compound in the U.S. base of Landstuhl, and 11 medical clinics in Ansbach, Baumholder, Brussels, Grafenwoehr, hohenfels, Kaiserslautern, SHAPE, Stuttgart, Vicenza, Vilseck, and Wiesbaden. A new project is underway to build a new military hospital in Landstuhl. *Goals: As detailed in this chapter, all services in those medical facilities must be designated as top priority targets to be attacked by our operators. The project of the new hospital must be stopped by all means available. Sleeping cells must work on destroying its maps, bribe contractors to withdraw from bidding, and inject the site where the building will be built with undetectable chemical injections.*

Ramstein: Ramstein Air Base or Ramstein AB is the United States Air Force Base in Rhineland-Palatinate, a state in southwestern Germany. It serves as headquarters for the United States Air Force in Europe. It has two runways, a drone war control center, a civilian mall, a travel agency office, military schools, a medical center and clinics, a movie theatre, TV and radio stations, and most importantly, a NATO military command center. *Goals: sleeping cells have a difficult task at hand; they must coordinate their efforts to work simultaneously to spread destruction all over this large base; details in this chapter are supported with maps.*

DoDEA (Department of Defense Education Activity) Europe division. Tasks: a group of your sleeping cells to work on disrupting the operating and demoralizing of the DoDEA (Department of Defense Education Activity) Europe division. DoDEA Europe operates 64 schools in 3 Districts in 8 countries across four time zones, and all must be taken down.

Another group of your sleeping cells to work on disrupting the Army & Air Force Exchange Service (Exchange) in Europe. Since the Exchange supports military morale, welfare, and recreation programs, disrupting its operations means losing income. Failure to support any of these programs will demoralize the U.S. military communities in Europe.

Also, work on disrupting services in libraries, theatres, post offices, food courts, malls inside U.S. bases, soldier barracks, community activity buildings, schools, and administrative services. Sleeping cells must maximize the results of their action, using whatever methods are needed to achieve their goals: hacking systems, bribing people, demolishing buildings, poisoning foods, and kidnapping people are examples of what they can do.

Attached are maps of the storage of weapons and dynamites, Dynamite *Baits, detonators, and directions to where destruction will occur.*

Meeting with the President of the United States

At this point, the Director of the National Intelligence Office asked the meeting to be adjourned until tomorrow. He nodded to the CIA, FBI directors, and the head of Operation Mitten to accompany him in his car. They all headed to the White House. When the CIA director asked why they were going to meet the President without waiting to verify the information in the books, the Director of the National Intelligence Office responded that he couldn't wait for that verification and that Congress might ask him later why he didn't inform the President once he knew about the Russian book. All then kept silent until they arrived at the Oval Office.

The President of the United States summoned the leaders of Congress and his National Security team and asked the Secretary of Defense to join the meeting. When all arrived at the Situation Room, the Director of the National Intelligence Office repeated the information he had previously presented to him. When finished, the President explained his issuance of an executive order to start an operation named Mitten, after a systems librarian discovered a pattern of Russian books with coded messages in them to start significant operations to destabilize European societies, demoralize U.S. troops in Europe, and disrupt services all over Europe. The President then updated the attendees on the progress of resolving the encrypted codes in the four books. Once all books are resolved, the actual execution of Operation Mitten will start, hopefully, end before the Russians start their operation. The President urged the CIA and FBI directors to verify the information as soon as possible, asked the Operation Mitten leader to speed up the phase of resolving all the encrypted codes in all books, and then put their final findings on his desk.

Big Bear, the Operation Mitten counselor, returned to the Cyber Room to review documents before going home to get some rest.

The next day, he started the meeting by informing the ex-Russian spies, Stacy, and his staff that the President of the United States appreciated their hard work but asked them to speed up their work, inviting the presenter of the next book to start.

Fourth Book – Russia Border States

Russia has land borders with five European Union states Finland, Estonia, Latvia, Lithuania, and Poland. Goals: Russia must maintain its influence, in particular, in Poland and the Baltic states, by seeking to limit its sovereignty. For example, the Estonian city of Narva is just a snowball's throw from Russia. More than 80% of Narva's residents are ethnic Russians. We must use the ethnic Russians in those five border states to achieve the Teremok operation goals. This book chapter has all the details for you, our supreme operator of the border states. Remember that the Russian President's order of the Teremok operation not to excluded Finland from any operational activities. Though this chapter is designed to be a part of the Teremok operation, it must be included and integrated into the strategic plan to stop the European Union's expansion eastwards.

Focus on the demoralization and destabilization of the military complex next to Bemowo Piskie, a village in northeastern Poland. The base is home to more than 15,000 Polish and NATO soldiers, and it's a stone's throw from Poland's borders with Belarus and the Russian enclave of Kaliningrad. Also, send your agents to Łask Air Base, where a detachment of the U.S. Air Force has been permanently based at Łask since November 2012. Additional units rotate to the base periodically to conduct training exercises. The force is considered nuclear-capable and has joined nuclear exercises with NATO. *We must punish Poland for offering to send its Soviet-made MiG29 fighter planes to Ukraine in conflict with Russia.*

In Romania, we must take down the Mihail Kogălniceanu Air Base near the Black Sea coast. Known as "MK," it has received millions of dollars in European Deterrence Initiative investment and hosts several hundred American troops on continuous nine-month rotations. The air base is at the southeastern edge of NATO, just a few hundred miles from Russia's Crimea.

Include both Finland and Sweden as priority operations. We have contacted the leaders to convince them to change their minds about joining NATO, but they refused. Execute this operation to the full extent, focusing on the border regions.

As far as Lithuania, revive the cells immediately scattered all over the country, activated the demolition plane to destroy the rail transit system that was created as part of the corridor deal to supply the Russian enclave Suwalki Gap, and blocked by the Lithuanian authorities after the start of the Russian special military operation in Ukraine. Give priority to this retaliation operation, and consider flying civilian planes through the Suwalki Gap to transport Russians and material to and from the Suwalki Gap, despite Lithuania's closure of its airspace. If NATO jets intercepted the civilian planes, Russian military units in the enclave have the authority to shoot them down.

All plans in this book must be supervised by top-level leaders and executed by supreme agents only.

Meet to Coordinate

The President of the United States hosted a secret meeting in the White House with the chancellor of Germany, the President of Poland, the head of NATO, the President of the European Commission, and the Mitten operation leader, the Big Bear. To their surprise, they found two generals, with complete uniforms, sitting at the meeting table. The President asked the generals to introduce themselves.

"I am Maksym Budanov, head of Directorate of Intelligence of the Ministry of Defense of Ukraine," The general told the attendees, adding: "Which conducts its activity in the military, political, technical, economic, signals, informational and environmental spheres, publishes the names and contact details of people it alleged were officers of Russia's Federal Security Service (FSB) involved in "criminal activities" in Europe." The general said, then gave a military salute to the attendees while facing the Ukrainian flag in front of him.

"And I am lieutenant colonel Piotr Krawczyk, head of the foreign intelligence agency of Poland. During the Mitten operation, we can assist in processing and forwarding information that may be significant to the security and international threat of the European countries, and decrypt the cryptographic communications of the Russian diplomatic missions and consulates around Europe."

Sitting next to the big bear, the Ukrainian general leaned on him, whispering a joke, "You don't seem to assemble that big bear in the Ukrainian Mitten fairytale, my friend." "But, we both are tough enough." Replied the operation leader with a big laugh.

"If we are done joking around, then let me talk about why we are here." Said the US President, then explained, in brief, the findings of the Russian operation and ongoing preparation for Operation Mitten by a joint team of U.S., NATO, and many of the European intelligence communities. The German Chancellor said he was informed of both operations and sent a team of top intelligence agents in his German Federal Intelligence Service, which is directly subordinate to his office, to participate in Operation Mitten. The head of the European Commission said she directed the director of the European Union Intelligence and Situation Center (EU INTCEN) to participate in the operation and added that the Center could share sensitive information among the external intelligence services of France, Germany, Italy, the Netherlands, Spain, and Sweden. She added that hundreds of agents from the European Common Identity Repository were information about all refugees coming to Europe and have been assigned to participate in the operation to provide all needed records of suspected infiltrators.

The President of the United States expressed his gratitude and satisfaction with the degree of supplying arms and financial help to Ukraine. He thanked the French, Poland, and Romanian Presidents and the Italian Prime Minister, saying all showed in the last few months signs of leadership in dealing with Russia, frequently meeting with the Russian President to convince him to withdraw from Ukraine and delivering harsh warnings to the Russians if they continued their aggression. The President expressed a special thanks to the Ukrainian president for agreeing to participate, to the full extent of Ukraine's available security resources, in the operation of Mitten.

Countdown

The next phase of Operation Mitten had two parts that would be executed simultaneously, explained the DNI Director in the preparation meeting that followed the resolving of the encrypted codes and messages in the four Russian books. The first step of part one was to put close surveillance on places, such as the Ukrainian border exits with European countries, publishing houses of the Russian books, banks, Russian embassies, and consulates in Europe, and to secure all the places mentioned in the books as possible targets by the Russian operation. All movements, even the little ones, must be recorded and analyzed. The second step in that part one was to put tight surveillance on people, not only the sleeping cell members mentioned in the books, but their extended families, friends, and friends. The director mentioned that our U.S. spies inside the Russian counterintelligence agency were mobilized to provide us with the latest movements. Government satellite surveillance would monitor the Ukraine borders and scan for any Chechens and other Russian agents who tried to cross the borders to Europe.

The second phase, the director said, would start when the President of the United States issues his order to execute it. In this phase, all people involved in the Russian operation would be rounded up, all places of weapons, money, explosives, embassies, consulates, and any place mentioned in the Russian books will be attacked, searched, and everyone in there would be arrested. Anyone showing resistance would be killed on the spot.

Once the President issued his order, the director added, a state of emergency would be imposed. All U.S. airports, ports, rail, and metro stations will be closed. All NATO and U.S. military bases would be put in Force Condition High, and all U.S. and NATO buildings would be on high alert. All U.S. naval ships, especially the ones carrying nuclear weapons, would be on high alert.

Ukraine, Japan, Australia, and the European Union, according to the operation plan, would file a case in front of the International Criminal Court against the Russian President, his aides, and his government for the conduct of intervening with the sovereignty of the European States and terror acts against embassies on foreign soils.

Possible Exposure

The Terermok operation team, situated in a particular communication room, received a coded message from an operator in Kaiserslautern, Germany, about suspicious activities by a systems librarian working as a civilian in Sembach Kaserne. The operator, Valentina's father Dmitriy, said in his message that his daughter told him an officer in plain clothes visited the family of that systems librarian, named Stacy Wade, many times and stayed for a short period each time he visited. No more information at this time, the operator said in his message. Still, he noticed Stacy Wade's TDY took longer than usual, and his family had no idea precisely what his temporary duty order was and where he went.

The message was escalated immediately to Valery, who called Alexandrovich Vasilyevich, Chairman of the National Antiterrorism Committee, and woke him up in the middle of the night to let him know about the possible exposure of Operation Teremok. Vasilyevich told Valery to contact the chief operator in the area and ask for verification and confirmation of the information included in the message. Both agreed that the whole operation would be at risk if the information proved true.

The CIA director's wife woke him up in the middle of the night, saying his office director was waiting to talk to him in the living room. He asked his wife to take him to the office in the basement and please get them some coffee. The office director told his boss they received an urgent cable from one of their agents in Russia who was planted in Russia's Antiterrorism Committee and worked there as a staff. The cable said the agent heard talks about an American systems librarian's unusual activity in Sembach Kaserne.

The CIA director took his aide to the car and ordered the driver to head to the house of the Director of National Intelligence office (DNI). Wondering what brought him to that late hour of the night, the DNI director took the CIA boss and his aide to the office in his house. The CIA director asked his aide to repeat what was in the cable. Upon hearing that, the DNI director picked up the phone and called the White House. The President of the United States was already awake and received the call. After listening to the DNI director and pausing for a while, the President asked him to assess the current stage of Operation Mitten, telling him if they could deceive the Russians and gain some time to finish the operation, we would succeed. The DNI director asked the President to give him a few hours to gather his committee, do the assessment, and then notify him. The President agreed.

Back in the National Antiterrorism Committee office, where an urgent meeting took place, Alexandrovich Vasilyevich, the director, asked for an immediate assessment of the situation after receiving confirmation of the unusual activities of Stacy Wade and his interview by the Wiesbaden intelligence officers. Valery Gerasimov, the Operation Terermok leader, said that everything is going on time, and all agents are in place with their instructions to execute the operation once they receive the green light, which is supposed to happen in two weeks. He added that if they speed up the decision-making process, he can start his operation a week earlier, but it is all up to the Russian President, who will give the final OK.

To deceive the Russians, the DNI, CIA, and FBI directors, along with the Secretary of Defense, agreed to send Stacy Wade and Lisa Ortiz back to Germany, telling them to perform their duties as usual and provide fake reports on imaginary missions they conducted during their TDY. The IMCOM director and Stacy Wade's and Lisa Ortiz's supervisors will be notified to assist in the cover-up.

Briza, Omar, and Robert were surprised and happy when Stacy opened his apartment door with his key, saying he was back. He was not surprised to see Valentina and her parents were there, and he showed no reaction. He told them how he and his colleague Lisa caught COVID-19 and were forced to be isolated for two weeks in a

U.S. base in the Netherlands. Valentina's parents looked at each other with no comments, which Stacy noticed.

The Netherlands base commander received instructions to issue the necessary COVID-19 isolation and release documents for Stacy and Lisa and mail them through the regular military mail to their addresses in Germany to fool the Russian operator and tell his people in the Russian Teremok communications room of Stacy's COVID 19 contraction and isolation, to make them believe everything was normal, with no exposure of the Teremok operation.

Omar introduced his girlfriend, Roksolana, to his father, saying they shared the same values. She believed in him and was sure he would be a successful businessman. Roksolana added they shared the same views about the war in Ukraine and were deeply involved in helping the Ukrainian refugees arriving in Kaiserslautern. Stacy told her that Omar was exceptional and asked her to take care of him. Omar told his father another piece of good news: His friend, Konstantin, said that Pavel Arseny, his father, had come back from Russia. Briza took Stacy to their room and asked him about Lisa; the librarian was with him on his mission. Stacy was surprised that Briza knew about Lisa, then guessed that Valentina's parents, the Russian operators, had told her. He explained to Briza that he was unaware that Lisa was assigned to the same TDY, and she helped him a lot during the mission, adding that Lisa also contracted COVID-19 during their mission. Still, Briza was not convinced.

When Stacy returned to his office, his colleague Sue Cox told him they were preparing for the next training for all library managers and supervisors the following week. She wanted him to give a presentation about his trip, adding that Lisa Ortiz agreed to co-present with him. Stacy asked his supervisor to cancel that presentation. When Stacy gave no reasonable excuse for the cancellation request, the supervisor gave the go-ahead for the presentation. Stacy then called the office of IMCOM HQ in Sembach, asking to meet Mr. Weise, the Director urgently. When Stacy told the director of the situation, Mr. Weise said this would be a good chance for Stacy and Lisa to erase any suspicion about their trip. He advised Stacy to fake a presentation about an imaginary temporary duty order with Lisa.

Sitting behind Lisa Ortiz during the librarian's training, Andy Walker, the envious coworker, heard Lisa telling Sue Cox that she and Stacy had spent some very intimate times during the TDY. He went outside, called his wife, and told her what he had just heard. He asked his wife to call or visit Briza, Stacy's wife, and tell her about Lisa's affair with Stacy.

Briza was devastated when hearing about the affair. She called her friend, Steven's wife, Norma, to tell her what happened, and asked if she could stay at her home until she divorced Stacy. Steven called Stacy and told him about Briza's knowledge of his affair with Lisa and that Briza was on her way, alone, to his house. Stacy was surprised and went angrily to Lisa. He asked her if they could talk outside and then told her what had happened. She was shocked and told Stacy she had just whispered about it to Sue Cox during the training. Stacy told her she was not a responsible person and could jeopardize his personal life and the ongoing operation. He told her she must go back to the Netherlands right away and not to talk to any person until he reported what happened and waited for instructions. Stacy called his brother back and asked him to calm Briza down and keep her in his house until we finished what we needed to do. Steven understood, telling Stacy he would take care of that.

The Operation Terermok team, situated in a particular communication room, received a new coded message from an operator in Kaiserslautern, Germany, about suspicious activities by a civilian systems librarian working in Sembach Kaserne. The operator said, in his message, that he was wrong in his suspicions and that everything looked normal in Germany, and he apologized for sending the previous message. Valery showed a sigh of relief, telling his team to resume the preparation of the execution of Operation Teremok as scheduled. He called Alexandrovich Vasilyevich, Chairman of the National Antiterrorism Committee. Valery notified him of the latest correspondence from their operator in Germany, adding that the preparation for Operation Teremok had resumed. The Chairman was pleased to hear the good news and told Valery he would call the Russian President to tell him the news.

Time to Round-Up

A summer heat wave blanketed Washington in mid-July; the President of the United States took his family to Camp Davide right after the 4th of July celebrations to spend the rest of the month there. While walking alone in Camp David, an aide came running to him with a secured phone. The DNI director was on the other side of the call. He notified the President about the end of the first and second steps of part one of Operation Mitten: surveillance on places, such as the publishing houses of the Russian books, banks, Russian embassies and consulates in Europe, and all the places mentioned in the books as possible targets by the Russian operation. All movements around those buildings, even the little ones, were recorded and analyzed. The director added that tight surveillance was in place on people, including the sleeping cell members mentioned in the books and their extended families, friends, and friends. The DNI director added that agents, troops, drones, planes, and navy ships all surrounded those places and people to ensure no one or piece of equipment would escape. The President was pleased to know that all European intelligence community organizations, NATO, and the United States intelligence community coordinated well in this operation. The President said he would wait two more days until the end of July. If he did not hear from the DNI director of any requests for delay, cancellation, or exposure of the operation, he would call the Congressional leaders to Camp David and issue his order to execute the final part of the operation: round-up.

Stacy, Briza, Omar, Robert, and Zlata, Omar's girlfriend, returned the visit to the Dmitriy Kirill family. Stacy was instructed to keep a warm relationship with the Kirill family to report their suspicious activities. The Kirills didn't seem very happy to see the visiting Stacy and his family, and they didn't complain. Valentina came from her room and sat beside Robert, giving Zlata a dirty look.

Daria cleared her throat and looked at Stacy with a smile,

"so, how was your last mission Stacy? We heard you were on a special military mission," she said. He looked at his wife and then at her.

"Well... it wasn't that special. Just helping the military library monitor some books." He said with a smile. She suddenly seemed more interested.

"Books? Isn't that boring?" she asked.

"it depends on its content; some books these days carry a lot of information," Stacy said again with a knowing smile. Dmitriy's wife, Daria, paused, unsure whether to be worried because of how he was smiling.

"Why are you smiling like that?" she asked. Stacy looked at her with one brow raised.

"Is there something you'll like to tell me?" he asked. Daria blushed lightly and looked away from him

"Oh, you are a funny man."

Before anyone else could talk, a loud knock on the door started; when Dmitriy opened it, a group of U.S. military police and intelligence officers entered the house. The man at the front had a piece of paper with him.

"We have a warrant for the arrest of Mr. and Mrs. Kirill. He announced, in a loud, thick voice, for everyone to hear.

One of the officers read the order:

"Fedor Bogdan, you are charged with a long list of war crimes, starting with espionage during a war."

Valentina jumped in anger, screaming at the officer

"Why do you call my dad Fedor? His name is Dmitriy" she didn't get an answer from her stupefied parents, so she turned to her mother, but noticed that her mother put her head down, looking into the floor to avoid Valentina's eyes.

The officer walked over to Valentina and gently put a hand on her shoulder.

"I am sorry, dear, Fedor Bogdan, or whatever name he gave to himself, is not your father. That woman, Daria, is not also your mother" Valentina looked at her parents with shock. There was some disbelief, too, as she couldn't bring herself to believe everything the officer had said. She became hysterical, collapsed, and started crying, and Zlata came to her side, feeling sorry for her. The officer added:

"They are Russian cells integrated a long time into the Kaiserslautern community," he said as he turned to the officers behind him.

"Please search the premises. Take them both to the car and keep them handcuffed. Have two officers standing guard over them" he then turned to the Kirills

"don't even try to run, you won't get far, and you would be exposing yourselves to danger. It is also pointless to try to contact the other sleeper agents. They are all being rounded up as we speak." If anything, their faces fell even more.

It didn't take long before Troops found a Russian-language book: *Terermok*. It was the main book addressed to the supreme Russian operator. They also found the digital version of the book on his laptop and his phone; they also found its online version. Stacy was not surprised when he was told that the so-called Valentina's father, Dmitriy, was that supreme agent, and his fake wife acted as his assistant.

Robert was as shocked as Valentina and walked up to her and threw his arms around her.

"Mom... dad, we cannot blame her for her so-called parents' sins." He then turned to her and looked into her eyes affectionately.

"don't worry, honey... this doesn't change anything. I still love you. If you want, you can come with me when we return to America because ill apply for you to come to be with me."

The look of love in his eyes was returned with eyes full of hate and disgust. Valentina snickered.

"You are a dumb fool," she said.

"You think I cared about your crippled ass? You are nothing to me."

Again, she looked around, this time with a look of hardened defiance in her eyes.

"Мы вас похороним!"

She said as she hissed like a snake.

The lead officer who knew Russian turned to Stacy and the others and interpreted.

"We will bury you!"

Robert hung his head in shame. The intelligence officer told Valentina,

"Ma'am, you need to come with us too." As he slapped some handcuffs on her wrists. She didn't resist. She didn't even seem to mind.

While the agent was taking Valentina away, Omar's girlfriend, Zlata, said to her

"You deserve to be in jail for your black soul." Valentina hissed at her too.

Returning to their building, after the drama they experienced in Valentina's fake parents' home, they face yet another group of military officers and troops. Omar was in shock when he heard that the father of his Russian friend Konstantin got arrested, along with two of his oldest brothers, for being Russian agents, as they found a copy of the second book in the father's car and on his laptop. The officer in charge told Konstantin, who never was that close to his father, the actual name of the man who thought he was his father: "Serge Stanislav" The officer added that Serge had never been married, never had kids, and it was all a big lie by the Russian intelligent machine. Konstantin was in disbelief at what was happening in front of him. He started asking: "Who am I, why, how" Then he went into a coma.

Stacy and Stfan's families stood there silent, not finding words to say. They experience two completely shocking stories a few hours apart.

The third shocking story that left Stacy in disbelief was when he knew he was dealing all the time with one of the most notorious

Chechen Ramzan clans, Islam, who drove Briza and Robert many times in his van, and whose family Stacy had over dinner many times.

When Islam was interrogated, he was offered the option of not prosecuting some of his family members in exchange for providing all information he had about the sleeping cells in Europe, especially in Ukraine, how they functioned there, and how Russian agents embedded themselves with the Ukrainian refugees who arrived in Europe. Most importantly, he was asked to provide how he contacted the Russian spy agency and reported to it. At the end of the interrogation, he was instructed to send a final message, handled by the CIA agent: "From the Mitten operation's Big Bear to the Teremok operation's Russian characters: thank you for your cooperation. Next time, do not use a Russian fairy tale to guide you, as you can see it turned your operation into one of the most humiliating spy operations of all time."

Andy Walker came to work with a sad face and in a depressed mode. When asked by his colleagues about the reason for his strange condition, he told them that his wife, Ann, was taken from their home by U.S. military police for questioning and might face a trial because of her role in spreading military secrets and cooperating with foreign agents to harm U.S. national security. The government had to determine if she was maliciously in league with the Russians or, maybe even worse, just a useful idiot who made herself feel important with her loose lips. Either way, she was guilty of helping the enemy. Stacy told him how sorry he was, but he warned him many times to watch his wife and tell her to keep her mouth shut and to follow the strict way you, her husband, took in handling military information. "Instead," Stacy added with anger, "you and her went on your ways to insult my wife and me, accusing us of being jealous" Stacy pointed his finger at Andy while telling him, "I will never forgive your wife, Ann, attaching my wife the middle of the Mall by giving her quite a tongue-lashing after I stopped her continuous talk about Army matters when we met in

Kleber Kaserne" "now, I hope she gets what she deserved" Stacy ended, giving Andy Walker a death stare while turning to walk away.

Steven phoned Briza with the news that the operation was underway, explaining in detail his role and her husband's role in this operation and how Stacy and Lisa's fake relationship was part of deceiving Russian intelligence until the execution of the operation started. He added that now that the operation had started, her place was to be with her husband and boys at her apartment. Briza was in disbelief while hearing Steven's talk, and Steven told her to get ready, as they all were going to Kaiserslautern to be united with Stacy and the boys.

Briza hugged Stacy, crying, saying she was sorry for thinking he had an affair with Lisa, adding how proud she was for all that he and his brother did for the country. Later that day, Steven told Stacy he had to lie to Briza and told her that his affair with Lisa was fake and was a part of the operation. Steven warned Stacy not to do such a thing again, or he will tell Briza the truth. Stacy gave his brother his word that it would never happen again, how much he appreciated his brother's act that saved his marriage, and most importantly, his boys' faith in their father.

Zlata and her parents visited Stacy, Briza, and the boys to congratulate him. Stfan told Stacy that he and his wife decided to move to America to be close to their daughter, who chose to travel with Omar and stay with the Stacy family when they moved back to the States. Stefan said his request to be transferred to the Jacobs company HQ in Philadelphia had been approved, so he and his wife will find a house near Stacy's home.

"Well, I have a surprise for you all," Stacy replied. "Zlata, her mother, and my son Omar will be included in a European NGO delegation heading to Ukraine soon to meet with officials and tour the capital city of Kyiv." Zlata, her mother, and Omar were in disbelief and started hugging and jumping around, while Stfan shook hands with

Stacy, thanking him. Robert and Briza stood there just smiling and clapping. "Wait, there is more; silence and listen," Stacy added. "I was supposed to go with you, but I will not go for security reasons. Guess what you will meet when you are in the Ukrainian capital?" They all looked at each other, then begged Stacy to continue. "The President of Ukraine," Stacy announced in a loud voice. Screaming and jumping in joy, all in the room went into a state of joy. "How were you able to arrange that, my friend?" Asked Stfan. Stacy told him that part of operation Mitten of mobilizing the international Non-Governmental Organizations (NGOs) around the globe to help Ukraine in its struggle. "That's how I convinced the operation leader to form a delegate of those living in Germany and participated in efforts to help Ukrainian refugees travel to Ukraine. "Omar will receive from the Ukraine President on my behalf, let me read to you:" Stacy said while opening a letter and started reading: "Stacy Wade has been awarded the Distinction of the President of Ukraine for the Defense of Ukraine, which is awarded usually to soldiers and employees of the Armed Forces of Ukraine, staff of intelligence agencies who took a direct part in the implementation of measures necessary to ensure the defense of Ukraine, in the implementation of actions to secure the defense of Ukraine protecting the population's security and interests of the state in connection with the large-scale armed aggression of the Russian Federation against Ukraine."

Stacy then told all the latest news. His family's stay in Germany was over as the Army terminated his contract. The DoD offered him a new job at the Pentagon as the head of a newly created department of DoD library systems.

In Frankfurt airport, Stfan, Stacy, Briza, and Robert waited for the NGO European delegation members to come out of the international arrivals gate; among them were Omar, Zlata, and her mother, Roksolana.

Back in the apartment, Omar gave his father, the Ukrainian Distinction certificate and a letter from the President of Ukraine. Briza couldn't wait until Stacy opened the letter as she snatched it away from him and started reading loudly, "Dear Mr. Stacy Wade, I am sorry you were not able to come to Ukraine, as I understand the security concerns prevented you from coming. I would like to thank you for your role in discovering the Russian threat to European countries. Though we never met before, and we might not meet again, I am proud of the role we both played in assisting in the toppling of that Russian dictator, I saved my country, and you assisted in saving yours. In the end, both of us contributed to the fall of the Russian dictator. Thank you! Signed by the President of Ukraine," Briza kissed the letter, jumped in Stacy's arms, and gave him a big kiss. Omar hugged Zlata, Stfan kissed Roksolana, and Robert stood there smiling.

U.S. President Jokes

The President addressed the nation in a nationally televised speech. He told the country and the world about the Russian revenge operation of Terermok, how it was discovered by a devoted American who worked as a systems librarian in Sembach Kaserne in Germany, and how it was stopped before it started with a counteroperation named Mitten. He added that the U.S. intelligence community, NATO intelligence, and European allies' intelligence communities coordinated the preparation and the execution of Operation Mitten.

He assured the American people and the world that all people involved in the Russian operation were rounded up, all places of weapons, money, explosives, embassies, consulates, and any place mentioned in the Russian books were attacked, searched, and everyone in there was arrested.

The President added he was pleased to learn that the Russian dictator was deposed by his generals but promised not to rest until those generals and all those involved in the Teremok operation and the war in Ukraine were brought to justice to join the Russian dictator in the Hague prison. He said that the United States of America and its allies reported, with evidence collected by officials and citizens around the world, the Russian plot to the International Court of Justice (ICJ) to bring all those who were involved in the Russian operation to conduct war crimes against American and European citizens in Europe.

He joked that if Moscow chose a name of a Russian fairy tale for its operation, we selected a name of a Ukraine fairy tale for our operation. He added that, while he spoke, the American ambassador to the Hague presented the ex-Russian Russian with a copy of the Ukrainian book "Mitten" with no encrypted codes.

A Story to Write

Above the glove compartment area, inside the shuttle that was taking them to Frankfurt airport, there was a book. It was a Russian fairy tale written in English. When Stacy Wade opened his eyes, he looked around him, noticed the book, grabbed it slowly, went through its pages in disbelief, and then looked at the driver, trying to remember who she was. Then a hand touched his shoulder. When he looked back, it was his wife, Briza, talking to him. He was shocked to see her, and when he turned his eyes around the van, he saw his oldest son, Omar, holding hands with a young girl, and his youngest son, Robert, sitting quietly and looking sad. Briza had to shake him a little to wake him from his condition, asking him what was wrong with him. After composing himself, he seemed still in no-belief mode. He confusingly asked where they were and where they were heading. All the people in the van, except him, laughed loudly. Then Briza told him they were returning to America after his contract with the U.S. Army ended.

Stacy looked around again; once he noticed Omar's girlfriend, he smiled and said, "Hi Zlata," The girl looked around, confused. "Are you saying hi to me, Mr. Wade?" "Her name is Nancy, dad," Omar intervened. Stacy, realizing he was still under the influence of the Russian fairytale, said he was sorry to take Nadia for someone else. When they arrived at the airport, Stacy asked the driver how that book ended up in front of him. The driver, a fluent English-speaking woman, said the book was hers, as her husband is a German of Russian origin, and he loves Russian fairy tales. She read the book during her breaks, told Stacy, and added she noticed him listening to the news of the Russian invasion of Ukraine. While reading the book during the van's three-hour trip from Kaiserslautern to Frankfurt airport, he dropped it and looked like he was daydreaming about something during the rest of the trip.

Once Stacy and his companions settled inside the plane, he told Briza, who sat next to him,

"I am thinking of writing a story when we are settled back in America."

"A story, you want to write a story? About what?"

He answered: "Sembach."

About the Author

Said Shafik works at the US European Command's IMCOM. A systems librarian manages the library systems for all US Department of Army MWR libraries worldwide, and supports NATO libraries as well. Read more at https://sembachbook.com/.